"With an interesting location, compelling characters, and lots of Christmastime charm, Liz Johnson has created a story that will sweep you right into the holiday spirit. And leave you craving a delicious slice of homemade pie!"

Melody Carlson, recipient of a *Romantic Times* Career Achievement Award; author of *A Royal Christmas*, *Second Time Around*, and *The Happy Camper*

"*Meddling with Mistletoe* is the perfect book to get you in the holiday spirit. Fans of Denise Hunter and Karen Kingsbury will be delighted with this Christmas romance that's akin to a Hallmark movie in book form."

Sarah Monzon, author of *All's Fair in Love and Christmas*

"*Meddling with Mistletoe* is the book you're wishing for this holiday season."

Angela Ruth Strong, author of *Husband Auditions*

Meddling with Mistletoe

Books by Liz Johnson

PRINCE EDWARD ISLAND DREAMS

The Red Door Inn

Where Two Hearts Meet

On Love's Gentle Shore

GEORGIA COAST ROMANCE

A Sparkle of Silver

A Glitter of Gold

A Dazzle of Diamonds

PRINCE EDWARD ISLAND SHORES

Beyond the Tides

The Last Way Home

Summer in the Spotlight

Meddling with Mistletoe

Meddling with Mistletoe

A RED DOOR INN
Christmas Romance

Liz Johnson

a division of Baker Publishing Group
Grand Rapids, Michigan

Published by Revell
a division of Baker Publishing Group
Grand Rapids, Michigan
RevellBooks.com

Printed in the United States of America

Library of Congress Cataloging-in-Publication Data
Names: Johnson, Liz, 1981– author.
Title: Meddling with mistletoe : a Red Door Inn Christmas romance / Liz Johnson.
Description: Grand Rapids, Michigan : Revell, a division of Baker Publishing Group, 2024.
Identifiers: LCCN 2024006048 | ISBN 9780800744885 (paperback) | ISBN 9780800746407 (casebound) | ISBN 9781493447213 (ebook)
Subjects: LCGFT: Christmas fiction. | Romance fiction. | Christian fiction. | Novels.
Classification: LCC PS3610.O3633 M43 2024 | DDC 813/.6—dc23/eng/20240220
LC record available at https://lccn.loc.gov/2024006048

Scripture quotations are from the King James Version of the Bible.

This book is a work of fiction. Names, characters, places, and incidents are the product of the author's imagination or are used fictitiously. Any resemblance to actual events, locales, or persons, living or dead, is coincidental.

Cover illustration: Nate Eidenberger
Cover design: Laura Klynstra

Published in association with Books & Such Literary Management, BooksAndSuch.com.

Baker Publishing Group publications use paper produced from sustainable forestry practices and postconsumer waste whenever possible.

24 25 26 27 28 29 30 7 6 5 4 3 2 1

Behold, a virgin shall be with child, and
shall bring forth a son,
and they shall call his name Emmanuel,
which being interpreted is, God with us.

Matthew 1:23

For the dreamers without a dream.
For the ones unsure what to long for,
the ones afraid to hope.
You are seen.
You are loved.
You are not alone.

one

IT WAS THE BEST OF TIMES, it was the worst of times.

And she was definitely in the wrong Dickens story. Because this was really, very much the worst of times. At least the worst possible time for her house to fall apart. Not even the shimmering snow swirling outside the window and the scent of the real pine tree in the living room could transport her into old Bob Cratchit's kitchen.

With a grunt, Whitney Garrett kicked her oven door closed and threw herself against the stovetop. The downright chilly stovetop. The one that should have been toasty warm by now since she'd turned the oven on to preheat twenty minutes before.

Resting her head on her crossed arms, she groaned in the direction of the nearest burner.

It probably didn't work either.

The stupid oven had been on the fritz for months. But she'd thought it would hang on at least a little while longer. Just through the Christmas season. That was all she needed. Five weeks. That was not too much to ask.

Except, apparently it was.

She kicked the white metal frame and promptly screamed as her big toe throbbed. Stumbling toward the adjacent counter, she hopped on one foot until the pain subsided.

Letting out a soft sigh, she stared at the three pies—uncooked as they were—sitting on her counter. All apple cherry with precise lattice tops and rippled rims. But they were missing the golden color and rich scent that made everyone's mouths water.

She shot one more scowl at her broken appliance for good measure.

Whitney had called her landlord, Craig, about getting the oven looked at a week ago. He'd stopped by and fiddled with something near the pilot light. And it had worked for exactly five days.

He'd done the same thing with her washing machine the summer before. It had lasted for three weeks. Craig was one of those guys who insisted on being the first line of defense. He wouldn't pay for a repairman until he'd tried to fix it himself.

Picking up her phone, she punched in Craig's office number. It rang and rang, and no amount of tapping her toe made him answer. She was just about to hang up when his voicemail kicked in.

"Hey, this is Craig. The missus and me are in the Maldives for our fortieth anniversary. Leave me a message, and I'll get back to you when we get home the middle of December."

Whitney put her phone on the counter and glared at it. "Seriously?"

Craig was literally halfway around the world and clearly not checking voicemails. For three weeks. Those were weeks she couldn't spare. Not when she could bake only a couple pies at a time. And when she'd already paid for her stall at the Summerside farmers' market in two weeks.

Staring at her phone for a long moment, she debated her next move. She snatched it up and put it back down just as quickly.

Just call them.

No.

Maybe they'll change their minds.

Her fingers brushed her phone before she yanked them back. Her dad had been more than clear.

But these are extenuating circumstances.

Every other absolute failure had had extenuating circumstances too.

Her parents weren't going to bail her out of another harebrained scheme—and she'd had many of them. Even though she'd fully thought through her plan to attend the culinary institute in the spring, if things fell apart, she'd already used up every single favor a daughter could ask for.

With a huff, she pushed her phone across the rust-colored counter and turned to the pies, already picturing the way the cherries would bubble and turn the apples bright red. She just needed a place to cook them.

An image flashed across her mind. Double ovens built into the wall. Stainless steel. Meticulously maintained. Enough room for even the biggest Christmas feast.

The very best place to cook in North Rustico was Rose's Red Door Inn. Everyone knew Caden Holt Jacobs's kitchen was charmed. Maybe it was Caden who brought the magic.

Whitney had certainly thought so as a high school student learning to cook from the inn's chef herself. Maybe Caden had left some fairy dust behind. And the inn was closed this time of year—really any time of year that threatened frost.

Which meant . . .

Whitney barely dared to hope. But it was her only chance to save her stall at the farmers' market. To save her business this season.

After carefully tucking the pies into her fridge, she pulled on her thick jacket and tied her scarf around her neck. Wind whipped inside when she opened the kitchen door, but she stepped into the ankle-deep snow and hurried along the path toward the big blue house with the bright red door.

Whitney let the warmth of the inn's mudroom fully embrace her before loosening her homemade blue scarf. Thumping her boots on the floor, she knocked off as much snow as she could, but not enough to risk tracking it beyond the tiled floor. So she toed off each fur-lined boot and crept into the kitchen.

The inn was oddly silent. At least upstairs. The echo of children's play seeped through the floorboards, shrieks of laughter and delight. But Marie and Seth Sloan, proprietors of Rose's Red Door Inn for nearly ten seasons now, didn't seem to be around.

Whitney tiptoed through the immaculate kitchen, giving the stainless-steel double oven an envious glance before making her way down the short hall to the office. The big wooden door stood wide open, revealing a desk piled with papers in nearly every color of the rainbow. The sleek computer monitor was on, but the little room was empty.

She turned back to the kitchen and stopped mid-stride.

Chubby cheeks and a near-toothless grin greeted her from

the hardwood floor. Squishy hands grabbed at the air as the baby reached up. "Nee-nee. Nee-nee."

Whitney scooped up the little doll, pulled her into a tight hug, and pressed a kiss to her silky brown hair. "Well, hello there, Miss Jessie. Where's your mama?"

The little girl blew a series of bubbles in response and giggled with glee, her rosy cheeks positively pinchable.

"Should we go find her?"

Jessie blew some more bubbles, which Whitney took as agreement, and they trotted around the rest of the main floor. Decorating had already begun in the parlor, which featured an evergreen in the corner, adorned with ribbons and bows and strings of popcorn. A warm fire crackled in the hearth, a cozy blanket laid across the oversized chair. It looked ready to welcome any and all guests.

Except the inn was officially closed. It wouldn't open up again until tourists returned in May.

Suddenly a cry split the air. "Jessie. Je-essie!" Footsteps pounded down the back stairs, and Whitney raced to meet them in the kitchen.

"She's here. She's fine."

Marie landed on the bottom step with a sigh of relief, swinging her mass of brown waves out of her face as she put her hands on her hips and frowned at her youngest. "Her brother thinks it's funny to take her downstairs and then promptly forgets about her."

Whitney chuckled. That sounded about right.

Only then did Marie seem to realize she hadn't even greeted her visitor. "I wasn't expecting company today," she said, giving Whitney a quick side hug. "How are you?" She offered a smile that hadn't changed much since they'd met so many years ago. Perhaps there were a few new wrinkles around her eyes, but if she had any gray hairs, she hid them well. "Would you like a cup of tea?"

Whitney flashed hot beneath her puffy coat, but she nodded anyway. "Please."

Marie set about putting the copper kettle on the gas stove before wiping her forehead with the back of her hand. "You can pick your flavor." She nodded toward the cupboard. Whitney knew it well.

But when she pulled the metal tea box down, it was suspiciously light. She flipped open the lid to discover exactly one package—a sleepytime tea.

Marie's entire face went red. "Oh no. I'm so sorry. I thought I had . . . I guess I need to add that to my list. I'm just . . ." She rolled her eyes at herself. "I can't seem to keep up with anything right now. The kids. The house. The guests."

Jessie began to squirm at the stress in her mom's voice, and Whitney bounced her until she calmed down. "Guests?"

Marie opened another white cupboard and produced two white packets. "Will instant hot cocoa do?"

Whitney nodded, her eyebrows still pinched together. "What guests? Aren't you closed?"

"We should be. But Aretha needs a favor, and you know I can't say no to her." Marie swiped at a frizzy curl, suddenly looking more unraveled than she had just a moment before. "So now I have two guests checking in in a week, a Christmas pageant to direct, and I promised Little Jack that we'd make gingerbread houses and go see the lights. Plus, I'm supposed to host the cookie exchange this year, and I need to buy presents for the kids. Seth too, I suppose."

The way she tacked her husband's name on as an afterthought made Whitney chuckle, but the deep lines of stress around Marie's mouth quickly sobered her.

This was the worst time to beg for a favor—yet Marie was the only person she could think to ask. If her parents hadn't just moved into the condo in Charlottetown, she'd have asked to borrow their oven. Borrowing an appliance wasn't quite like being bailed out. It was just a little bit of assistance.

But her mom and dad were tucked into their cozy two-bedroom along the harbor, where they insisted they would revel in their pension years.

And if all went as planned, she'd be moving to Charlottetown shortly after the first of the year too. That just didn't solve her immediate dilemma.

Whitney pressed the tip of her thumb to the corner of her mouth and chewed gently on her nail, which tasted suspiciously like cinnamon. She frowned at her finger, and Jessie seemed to giggle at her problem.

Fine. That earned the little cherub a one-way trip to the floor. Which was apparently not punishment. Jessie scooted across the floorboards, opened the first cupboard she encountered, and immediately pulled plastic containers and their mismatched lids to the floor.

"I'm sorry." Whitney rushed to retrieve Jessie, but Marie stopped her with a hand to the arm.

"Don't worry about it. Jessie has long since decimated whatever organizational system Caden had in place in those bottom shelves. Better she's making a mess in here than exploring the Christmas tree again." Marie released a long-suffering sigh, pairing it with a smile that looked a lot like love for her youngest.

As she stirred the cocoa mix into two steaming mugs,

spoon clanking, Marie looked over her shoulder. "So, what brings you by?"

"Oh, um . . ." Whitney was unable to form even the most basic words, her tongue having lost its way.

Marie held out one of the green mugs. The ring around the base was clearly the island's famous red clay. It was probably from Mama Potts's Red Clay Shoppe. Marie sold their plates and platters, bowls, and other dishes to guests all summer long.

Whitney wrapped her fingers around the warmth of the mug and inhaled the sugary steam. The sides of the cup were just a little bit uneven, a testament to the way each piece was crafted by hand.

From her place tucked into the corner of the counter, Marie raised her eyebrows as she sipped her own drink. "Are you all right since your folks moved? Are they doing okay?"

"Oh. Yes. They're great. They're . . . I guess they really like living in the city."

Marie's dark eyebrows dipped together over her perfect nose. "I haven't seen you at church the last couple weeks. Is everything . . ."

"I've been selling my pies at farmers' markets around the island."

Marie's face relaxed, and she blew into her mug, sending steam spiraling.

"But that's . . . kind of why I'm here." Whitney released the last words in a quick stream, still afraid to ask, yet terrified not to. She couldn't back out now. "My oven broke. Again. And I can't make more pies if I don't have an oven. And I need . . ."

Her mom had always said that it was uncouth to talk about money. But she needed it.

The Culinary Institute of Canada in Charlottetown had

no problem talking about money. And asking for it. And reminding her that if she wanted her spot to remain reserved, she needed to make a payment. That just wasn't going to happen without an oven—a fully functioning one at that.

"Oh, Whitney. I'm sorry about your oven. How can we help?"

Great. Marie was going to make her say the words. It would only take five of them. But really, couldn't she just offer?

Whitney took an unsteady sip of her cocoa. It was watery and fairly flavorless, but at least it gave her something to do while she stared at the floor and plucked up all her courage. "Maybe . . . if it wouldn't be too much trouble . . . would it be okay if . . ."

Marie's eyebrows pinched all the way together, confusion clearly written across her face.

Taking a deep breath, Whitney closed her eyes and opened her mouth and prayed that the words that came out would make sense. "Would it be okay for me to maybe use the inn's oven to bake my pies?"

"Oh." Marie's mouth hung open, her eyebrows raising nearly to her hairline.

The silence between them fell heavier than a blanket of wet snow, and Whitney rushed to fill it, but Marie beat her.

"I mean, I'd love to help you out. It's just . . ." Her arm waved toward Jessie happily clapping pan lids together like cymbals. "It's such a . . ."

Busy time.

Marie didn't need to fill in the words. The whole island was nearly buzzing in anticipation of Christmas and all the activities the season held. And Marie's season was going to be extra full.

After struggling so much to find the words only minutes

before, Whitney had no trouble spitting out a wholly unexpected trade. "I could watch your kids while you have guests."

She was certain she looked as shocked as Marie in that moment. She liked Marie and Seth's little ones more than any others in their little hamlet, but she didn't know much about caring for kids. Her own sister was only eighteen months younger, and there were no nieces or nephews in the family yet.

The offer hung there like week-old laundry on the line, nearly forgotten but refusing to be ignored.

A slow smile stretched across Marie's face, her eyes lit by a flame within. "Really? That would be amazing. Even a few hours a day—like when I'm at the church for rehearsals or going shopping. Seth has been focused on a remodeling job in Cavendish, and he's trying to wrap it up before Christmas. He's been leaving early in the mornings. And we agreed to the job before Aretha told us about her guests." Marie sighed as though she'd set down a heavy weight. "Do you truly have time?"

A glimmer of hope flickered inside. Whitney didn't have time not to, so she nodded quickly. "Sure thing. I'd be happy to."

"And you would just need to borrow the oven?"

Hesitating to stretch the request, Whitney swallowed softly. "And maybe the kitchen to do some prep." Caden had top-notch tools that could make her even more productive.

Marie took a step forward, resting her mug on the island. "And maybe cook some breakfasts?"

Her mouth went dry, and no amount of sipping rapidly cooling cocoa could change that.

"The Lord knows Caden is a wonderful teacher, but she hasn't taught me squat." Marie chuckled. "Nearly ten years of friendship and I can barely cook scrambled eggs. I'd like to be able to offer our guests a little something more."

"You want me to fill in for Caden?" Whitney began shaking her head to answer the question before she had even finished asking it. "I don't think I'd be . . ."

Marie slipped around the edge of the island and leaned in close. "But you're a natural. And you were part of Caden's first class of summer school students. I'm not asking for much. There are only two guests. It doesn't have to be elaborate. Simple. Edible."

"So, if I watch the kids and make breakfast, I can use the whole kitchen?"

Blue eyes flashing bright, Marie nodded. "Please."

This wasn't exactly how she'd planned to spend the Christmas season. Then again, she hadn't really made *any* plans. She had booked farmers' markets and festivals all the way up until December 22. Then, if the roads were clear, she'd venture down to the city to see her parents.

Suddenly the next five weeks stretched before her, all bags of flour and cups of sugar, fresh fruit and warm pies.

Just her. And some pastries.

Jessie pulled a pot from the cupboard, and it crashed to the floor, making both women jump. Setting down her mug, Whitney scooped up the little girl and looked at her mom. This didn't have to be a lonely holiday season. And if spending the upcoming weeks helping at the Red Door meant access to Caden's kitchen, she couldn't possibly refuse.

"All right. I'll do it."

two

THE TINY PLANE with only one seat on each side of the aisle dipped forward, and no matter how quickly Daniel Franklin grabbed at his armrest, he still slammed into the seat in front of him. It probably had something to do with the mere breath of space between his kneecaps and the back of the blue chair. “Sorry,” he managed to mumble after the older woman in said seat groaned.

“Looks like we have a little bit of turbulence out there, folks.” The captain came over the intercom, sounding far too relaxed for someone in charge of a plane that was bouncing around like it wanted to drop out of the sky. “I’m turning on the Fasten Seat Belt sign a few minutes early, but we’ll be landing soon.”

The lone flight attendant did an unsteady dance down the aisle, collecting trash. After handing her his empty plastic cup, Daniel turned to the window and stared hard at the thick gray clouds that enveloped the plane. The wing sliced easily through them, and a few moments later, they broke free.

Everything beneath them was blue, peppered with the occasional whitecapped wave. And in the distance, the island. It was more white than famous red shoreline this time of year, and he scowled.

"She's beautiful, isn't she?"

He glanced over his shoulder at the flight attendant, who had stopped by his seat, her eyes fixed on the island below. Her question had most likely been rhetorical, but he couldn't help spitting out the truth. "I like her better when she's warm." At least, he had enjoyed summers on the island with his aunt Aretha when he was a kid.

"Oh? Not a fan of the cold?"

He wasn't really a fan of anything these days. But given the little green wreaths dangling from her ears, he had a feeling she might not appreciate that response. So he offered her a shrug before turning back to watch the island draw nearer. From his angle, he could see some of the Confederation Bridge—the thirteen-kilometer wonder that connected Prince Edward Island to the mainland. He'd been enamored with it as a kid, begging his dad to drive them over it.

It was still impressive, the way it broke up the ice flowing through the strait below. But it wasn't enough to keep his attention anymore.

As he bounced and jostled—even with his seat belt on—he turned back to the spreadsheets neatly stacked on the tray table before him. Rows and columns, formulas and equations. Spreadsheets made sense. Every time. And if they didn't, it was because there was a mistake.

Rooting out those errors made sense. Numbers made sense. Even the documents that Aunt Aretha had sent over in advance.

Sure, it was clear that the books had been done by some-

back surprised him, and it immediately became clear that Aretha's husband wasn't a casual hugger. Jack squeezed like he was in a contest he was determined to win. Daniel had no choice but to stand there—arms drooping at his sides—and be hugged.

"Haven't seen you since the wedding," Jack said as he finally stepped back. With a quick glance up and down, he added with a chuckle, "Have you grown since then?"

Daniel forced a mechanical grin. That's what nephews were supposed to do when their uncles made jokes like they were kids. Patting his trim waist, he shrugged. "No."

Jack's smile widened, deepening the many cracks and crevices of his face. "Well, you look good." Stooping to grab the handle of the suitcase, he said, "Let's get on the road before Aretha accuses me of keeping you all to myself."

Daniel silently followed Jack through the front door to the rust bucket parked just beyond the curb. Jack swung the suitcase into the truck bed like he regularly threw around heavy car parts, which he hadn't done since before he married Aretha, and then hopped behind the wheel.

Sliding onto the bench seat, Daniel closed the door on the cold and hoped the truck's heater worked. With a flip of his hand, Jack set the blowers going. Unfortunately, the air they threw out was colder than what was outside, and Daniel shivered despite his best efforts to remain still.

"It'll warm up in a minute," Jack said as he turned onto a two-lane highway. "Sure has been a cold winter. In Toronto too?"

Daniel wasn't sure if he was supposed to respond, but Jack gave him barely a second to before continuing his chattering.

"I keep telling your aunt we need to winter somewhere warmer. But she refuses to miss Christmas with the grands."

Daniel's eyebrows dipped as he tried to make sense of that term. Neither Jack nor Aretha had any biological children. And as far as he knew, they hadn't adopted any either. Lauren had had a dog that she called her mom's granddog, but Daniel didn't think Aretha would go that far.

"Grands?" he finally grunted.

Jack winked in his direction. "Seth and Marie's three."

Right. Jack's nephew and his wife, who had taken over Rose's Red Door Inn. Daniel had met them at the wedding, and Aretha's monthly emails had mentioned some kids. Though he usually couldn't remember how many or their ages. He could only retain a finite amount of information. The formulas and financial principles in his textbooks had been more important to hang on to.

Before Daniel could even confirm that he'd heard Jack, the older man rattled on. "Guess we're not technically grandparents, but we get all the benefits." His pale eyes flashed as he looked across the cab for a brief moment. "We get to babysit and read to them and get all the toddler hugs and giggles. And then give them back when it's time for a diaper change."

Jack chuckled like he was the first person to ever make that joke. Daniel offered an obligatory half smile.

"No, your aunt won't hear of leaving the island for the holidays." Leaning in like he had a secret, Jack added, "She complains about all the work it takes to decorate the inn, but honestly, I think she loves it. It's an excuse for her to spend time with Marie too."

Sure. But he hadn't been called all the way from Toronto to help decorate.

Jack sighed as the heater finally began pushing out lukewarm air. "Maybe we can go somewhere warmer after Christmas next year. Once the store is sold."

There it was. His whole reason for being on the tiny island. "She's really going to do it?"

Jack's never-ending smile dimmed, his gaze hard out the windshield. "I didn't believe her when she suggested it either. That store—I've never known her without it. It's got her fingerprints all over it. And it's become her trademark."

Aretha had started the store after his dad's brother had walked out on her—walked out of all their lives, actually. Their blood relative had disappeared, but Aretha had remained family. Always.

Her home had become his family's summer vacation destination—though Daniel had often questioned the child labor laws that allowed her to put him to work in the antiques store. Dusting and organizing. Sweeping and hefting whatever she needed him to move. When he'd been a little older, she'd taught him the books, showed him how to take inventory.

Of course, payment had always been a double scoop of Cows' Gooey Mooey ice cream. Still a better deal than some of the jobs he'd worked to put himself through school.

Shaking off the nostalgia, he sighed. He couldn't imagine Aretha Franklin without her store. It was as much a part of her as her famous introduction. "No relation to the singer."

Jack tapped the brakes as he turned north off the main highway, pine trees along the roadside giving way to white-washed fields peppered with colorful homesteads. "She'd never admit it, but her foot's still bothering her."

Daniel sat up a little straighter, his gut pinching. "I should have come back last summer."

"Ah, nothing you could've done." Jack waved him off, then with a shake of his head added, "Nothing any of us could've done. Doctor said it's healed the best it can after a break like that."

Still. He kicked himself for staying at school when Aretha had called last May. She'd laughed it off. "I dropped a bookcase on my foot. It was my own stupid fault, and there's absolutely nothing you can do for me here that you can't do in the city. Finish up your classes."

So he had. But now he worried that he might have missed a cue. Had he failed to read between the lines, misunderstood what she really needed? Lauren had said he usually did.

"Your aunt is just glad to have you here for the holidays. We've got a room all squared away for you at the inn."

He blinked slowly. "Not at your place?"

Jack's grin returned to its full force. "You're in for a treat. Marie almost never opens the inn outside of tourist season, but since we don't have room for both you and Ruby at our place, Marie said she'd make an exception." His bushy white eyebrows did a little jig. "Whitney is going to be cooking—and she's a far sight better than me."

His shoulders started knotting. "Who's Whitney?"

Whitney leaned into the warmth of the inn's oven, inhaling the sweet cinnamon-and-sugar crumble topping. It smelled like heaven, if she did say so herself. The crust was still pale yellow, and she rotated the pie 180 degrees.

"Almost there." She gave the top a little pat with her oven mitt, then nearly smashed her head on the top of the oven when the inn's front door slammed.

The kids!

She flung the oven closed and raced for the dining room,

where she'd left Little Jack and Julia Mae contentedly coloring twenty minutes ago. She glanced at the clock on the microwave above the stovetop—make that thirty! Flying against the swinging door, she expected to sail into the beautiful blue and silver dining room.

Instead the door abruptly stopped, and Whitney heard a loud grunt, then a louder crash.

No. No. No.

She froze, waiting for any sign that she hadn't maimed whoever had been on the other side. Like one of the kids.

Her heart jumped to her throat, and she gasped for air as she gingerly pressed her hand to the edge of the door. It gave a soft groan just as distinctly childish giggles filled the other room.

"That was funny! Do it again."

Definitely Little Jack.

A deeper chuckle joined in. Big Jack. "You okay there, son?"

Which meant the one she'd attacked was . . .

Pushing the door farther open, she peeked around the edge to find an unfamiliar man sprawled on the floor, leaning on one elbow and covering his forehead with his other hand. He squinted up at her through distinctly crooked glasses, one eye nearly all the way closed, a scowl firmly in place. The wooden chair next to him had been knocked to its side, and a wool peacoat—which had probably been hanging over the back of the chair—lay across the floorboards.

She stared at him for a moment. Then her gaze darted to the four-top beside the window where Little Jack knelt on a chair, crayon still in hand. Big Jack leaned over him, his hand resting on the seat back.

Whitney did a swift inventory of the room. "Where's Julia Mae? Did she go out the front door?"

Seth and Marie were going to kill her if she lost their middle child.

Ignoring the groaning man on the floor, she pushed the door against his foot until he moved it enough for her to slip through and dart toward the entryway. She already had the door handle in her grip when a sweet voice called from the hallway that ran past the parlor.

"Can I have a 'nack, Miss Whitney?" The little girl's dark curls bounced as she skipped from the powder room beneath the stairs.

Whitney was so thankful to see Julia Mae that she almost promised her a fresh pie of her choice. Instead, she knelt in front of her and wrapped her up in a hug. "Yes. Let's get you something to eat."

Her joy disappeared as she carried the little girl into the dining room, where both Jacks had helped the stranger to his feet. The stranger who could only be Aretha's nephew. The inn's guest.

And upright, he was a very handsome guest at that.

Her stomach did a full flip. This was not the introduction she had expected.

Then again, he didn't look like she'd expected either.

She paused, her lips pinching together as she tried to figure out what she'd thought he would look like. She hadn't exactly expected him to have Aretha's gray curls or pale skin. But she certainly hadn't thought he'd be so . . . well . . . much.

He was half a head taller than Jack, and his features were slim but filled out, like he was hiding an athletic build. His button-up oxford was open at the neck, the bowtie she'd expect on an accountant conspicuously absent. His wavy light brown hair was cut short on the sides but hung over his forehead. Behind the black rectangular glasses perched on his nose, his eyes were blue as ice. And just about as inviting.

Jack didn't seem to notice, a low rumble of humor in his chest preceding the slap he landed on the other man's back. "Well, that was exciting. Danny, this is Whitney. Whitney, Danny." Then, as though Whitney wouldn't put it together, he added, "Aretha's nephew."

"Daniel," he corrected, his voice deep, rough. It perfectly matched the glower on his face.

"I'm so sorry," she whispered. "I don't usually . . ." Her voice trailed off as she looked at the spot where he'd landed on the floor before dragging her gaze back up to meet his.

He stared at her for a long, silent second.

"I'm the temporary cook and nanny." She bounced Julia Mae in her arms in case he hadn't picked that up.

"Are you staying at my house?" the girl asked Daniel.

The corners of Daniel's mouth dropped even more—a feat Whitney hadn't been sure was possible—but he nodded.

"Papa Jack, are you gonna set up taco bed?"

Jack let out a snort of surprise, and Daniel's eyebrows nearly met, showing off two little concern lines.

Whitney quickly shook her head. "I think Mr. Daniel will get a real bed. In a real room."

Julia Mae frowned at that and looked about ready to argue.

Tugging on the little girl's chin, Whitney drew her gaze. "He's not just a friend." Daniel gave a soft grunt, and Whitney had to force herself not to make eye contact, certain he wouldn't stretch their acquaintance nearly that far. "He's a guest at the inn, so we'll treat him as such." She dipped her chin to give the girl a firm look.

With a wiggle and a frown, Julia Mae finally nodded.

Little Jack had been silent, his eyes wide with wonder as he looked up—and up—at Daniel. "I have bunk beds. You could stay in my room."

Daniel's eyes opened wide, his jaw slack, but before he could get anything out of his mouth, Whitney cut in.

"No, I don't think that's . . ."

Little Jack's hopeful smile began to droop, taking her spirits right with it. But she couldn't even entertain the idea. Marie had made it more than clear that Daniel was a guest. Even if Whitney had greeted him with a bruised nose.

At least it wasn't bleeding.

Suddenly the nose in question tilted to the side, and Daniel gave an audible sniff. "Is something burning?"

Whitney began to shake her head, but the distinct odor of burned sugar slapped her in the face. Her stomach dropped through the floorboards as she set Julia Mae down and raced for the kitchen. "My pie!"

She sighed as she pulled it free of the smoking oven. The beautiful crumb crust couldn't hide the berry-pink filling that had overflowed. Or the fact that she'd forgotten to put a pan beneath it. A perfect ring covered the bottom of the oven where the cinnamon and sugar had turned black.

A quick glance over her shoulder revealed that Jack, Daniel, and the kids were watching her every move. And surely questioning if she could manage to feed guests for the next four weeks without further disaster.

She offered a shrug of response to the curiosity painted across their faces. Just as the smoke detector began its incessant chirp.

three

DANIEL PRESSED a gentle finger to his tender nose and straightened his glasses one more time as the clothes in his suitcase swam before his eyes. The frames felt crooked no matter how many times he adjusted them.

That's what he got for thinking he could go into the kitchen unannounced. That's what he got for wanting a glass of water.

Whitney had been more than apologetic before bundling the kids in their winter coats and bustling them out the door, saying something about pageant practice and Marie already being at the church.

He hadn't followed most of what she'd said—probably because of the low-level throbbing behind his eyes. The glass of water he still hadn't gotten might help. With about three ibuprofen.

After shaking out a shirt, he hung it up in the closet next to a row of matching blue button-ups. Lauren had said they matched his eyes and he should wear them more. So he'd gone out and bought five. It made picking his daily outfit easy.

She'd been gone three years, but the shirts remained.

Most days they didn't remind him of her. Most days he put them on without even a flash of memory of her rolling eyes.

But seeing four matching shirts hanging in the closet—the fifth in the mirror's reflection—suddenly intensified his headache. He should find that water and a painkiller. Jack had left him to unpack and said he'd bring Aretha by later. He hadn't heard Whitney and the kids return with Marie. And Jack had said that Seth was working on a remodel about twenty minutes away. He'd told Daniel to make himself at home.

Daniel slipped the last of his neatly folded slacks into the drawer of the antique dresser that dominated the wall across from the king-size bed, zipped up his empty suitcase, and slid it onto the floor of the closet.

A quick check of the medicine cabinet in the adjoining bathroom proved fruitless. He was indeed going to have to make himself at home. Only at home, he knew where to find what he needed.

He stepped into the second-story hallway, then paused and listened. The house was silent save for the whistling wind outside, so he jogged down the stairs and made his way past the parlor, through the dining room, and into the kitchen.

The faint scent of burned sweets lingered, though Whitney had used a towel to wave the smoke out through the mudroom as soon as Jack had gotten the smoke alarm to turn off. Her eyes had been wild, nearly as uninhibited as her curly hair, as she'd held the guilty pastry at arm's length. The bright floral oven mitts hadn't made her look any less ridiculous.

As he looked around the white kitchen—clean, organized, spotless—it felt empty without Whitney.

He frowned. That couldn't be the case.

The entirety of their interaction had been a bruised nose and an overflowing pie. And the shocked expression on her face that had made him want to chuckle. He hadn't, of course. But sprawled out on the floor and staring up at her horrified face, he'd felt a humor bubbling in him that he hadn't known in years.

He didn't need that in his life.

Opening a top cupboard nearest to the sink, he peeked in to find stacks of white plates. He closed it and opened another. Matching bowls. And another. Spices.

Were they trying to hide the drinking glasses?

"Daniel?"

He slammed the spice cupboard closed like he'd been caught stealing from the cookie jar. Though he wasn't sure he'd risk eating a cookie from Whitney's kitchen. He'd seen no evidence that she wouldn't confuse salt for sugar—or worse.

He spun toward the familiar voice and tried not to look guilty as his aunt sashayed across the tile floor. Her gait was a little off, and she favored her right foot, just as Jack had said. But the strength in her embrace hadn't changed. She hugged him with her whole heart.

Her arms wrapped around his waist, and she rested her ear against his chest. He could literally feel her smile as her whole body vibrated with joy.

He tried to return the embrace with equal measure, but his heart wasn't half as big as hers. So he settled for a gravelly "Hi, Aunt Aretha," and a pat on her back.

"It's been far too long, my dear. I've missed you." She looked up at him, eyes glowing. "Promise you'll stay through Christmas."

Something in his stomach turned sour, but he swallowed against its rise in his throat.

"It won't be the same without you."

Right, because everyone knew the Grinch made Christmas special.

He forced half a smile for her anyway. "I'll stay as long as you need me."

Aretha sighed into him, giving him one more solid squeeze before letting go. "Oh, it is good to have you back on the island."

Only when she stepped away did Daniel look over her head of gray hair to see the woman standing in the doorframe. She was poised and statuesque, long legs encased in sleek black pants that disappeared into knee-high black boots. The heels had to add another three inches to her, but she stood as relaxed as if she was barefoot on a beach, hands in the pockets of her leather jacket and an easy red-lipped smile in place. Every single one of her blond hairs had been slicked back into a ponytail, as though there was a penalty for misbehavior.

"Oh, how rude of me." Aretha stepped toward the other woman, waving her closer. "Daniel, this is Ruby Lavoie—she's in acquisitions with Rogen & Reynolds. Ruby, my nephew Daniel Franklin."

He stepped forward, sticking out his hand out of habit more than greeting.

Ruby's smile brightened, and she shook his hand with a firm grasp. Professional and practiced.

"Ruby's from Toronto too," Aretha said with a little giggle.

He wasn't sure what the giggle meant, but he pushed on instead of asking. "Oh? I'm in Milton." Technically not in Toronto, but close enough for his aunt.

Ruby's smile dimmed slightly. "Yorkville."

That tracked. The woman was classy and sophisticated just like the affluent neighborhood near the University of Toronto. He couldn't afford to look at homes in that neighborhood even on his new CFO salary. Rogen & Reynolds paid well, apparently. Or she'd come from old money. Or both.

The throbbing behind his eyes picked up its pace, and he swallowed against his dry throat.

Aretha's gaze shifted back and forth between them. "Daniel just took a job as the CFO of All Terrain."

"The retail chain?"

He nodded. Chain was a strong word for the fourteen stores, but they wanted to expand, and he was going to help them do it.

"Oh, they're great. I have a friend there. Tunston Shaw?"

Daniel shook his head. "Haven't met him yet. I don't officially start until the New Year."

"Oh, I'm sure you'll meet him soon. We went to undergrad and grad school together. He's a sharp guy. And he says great things about the culture over there. I'm sure it'll be a good experience for you."

He nodded again, not sure how to respond. He never would have taken the job if he'd thought it might be a bad fit. The people he'd met seemed fine. But he wasn't taking the job to hang out with them. He was eager to do the work.

After a long pause, Aretha came to his rescue, offering a few facts about Ruby and her years at Rogen & Reynolds. Ruby was maybe a few years older than him, but her résumé sounded like she'd been in acquisitions and mergers since diapers. She didn't blush under Aretha's praise of her keen skills either. She just flashed her straight white teeth, all confidence and grace.

He was going to need to bring his A game when they started talking details.

Aretha had told him she'd received the deal points, but he had yet to see them. And he wasn't going to let Aretha get the short end of the arrangement.

He just had to figure out how to read what wasn't presented on the page. Ruby was all polish. Just like Lauren had been. And he'd never been able to read what she wanted—or what she needed.

He wasn't going to fall into that pit again. He'd find a way to figure it out. He had to.

Whitney had never felt so exposed as she did wearing jeans, an oversized cable-knit sweater, and one of Caden's aprons. Of course, her feelings had much more to do with the plated breakfast on the counter before her than what she wore.

She eyed the personal-size quiches, shaking the edges of the plates one more time to make sure the center didn't jiggle. Golden crusts. No sign of the overflow that had forced her to clean the oven the day before. The scent still lingered in the kitchen rafters, a cruel reminder of a stupid mistake and Jack's booming laughter. The kids had giggled too. But not Daniel. She hadn't been able to read the expression that had replaced his scowl.

Maybe she was so insignificant that he couldn't be bothered to notice her mistakes.

Scooping up the plates before her, she held her breath. If she'd messed up his breakfast, he'd certainly care about that.

By the time she made it to the swinging door, her hands trembled enough to send a ripe raspberry rolling from the simple dish of mixed berries, but it was too late to go back now. "Coming through," she called as she toed the door open an inch or two. When she was sure she wouldn't have a repeat of the day before, she pushed it far enough to slide through and was greeted by two grinning faces. And a third face displaying complete indifference, marred by the hint of a black eye.

Aretha's smile grew two sizes as Whitney slid the plates in front of Daniel and their other guest, a beautiful woman with sleek blond hair and the whitest teeth she'd ever seen.

Aretha sighed. "This smells divine."

Whitney pressed a hand to her stomach as it twisted into a hard knot. Marie had said she only needed to make breakfast for two. She could whip up another quiche, but it would take at least an hour. And by then, the other two would be long done.

"If Jack hadn't made my favorite ham and eggs this morning, you'd be going hungry." Aretha winked at her nephew, and if she noticed that Whitney let out a sigh of relief, she didn't let on.

Daniel responded to his aunt with a requisite grunt of acknowledgment but didn't move to eat his breakfast. Neither did his companion.

Maybe he'd warned the woman about the minor disaster the day before.

Nodding toward the blond, Aretha said to Whitney, "This is Ruby Lavoie. She works for the conglomerate in Toronto that's interested in buying the antiques store. Ruby, this is Whitney Garrett. She's filling in as the inn's chef."

With all the poise of a beauty queen, Ruby nodded her greeting. "Lovely to meet you. It looks delicious." But her hands stayed folded in her lap as wisps of steam dissipated before her.

"You too," Whitney said. "Enjoy your breakfast."

Daniel frowned—not angry but certainly perplexed. "A fork would help."

"A fork?" she echoed as her heart pounded in her ears.

Right. Utensils. A necessary part of eating most meals. She rushed to the kitchen to grab the rolled sets she'd left on the counter, delivered them, and returned to her haven without a word, praying the whole time that her cheeks hadn't turned as red as the ribbons on the tree in the parlor.

Her dad had raised her on Blue Jays baseball, and by her count she already had one strike at the inn. And it was only her second day.

Marie hadn't said anything to her that morning about the smoke alarm or the near-fire. But the kids weren't likely to keep it to themselves. She'd been surprised they hadn't announced it to their mom the moment they arrived at the church for rehearsal.

Forgetting utensils was more a ball than a strike, but they all added up. And she needed a home run to maintain her relationship with the stainless-steel wonders tucked into the wall beside the gas stovetop.

Running her hands over her unruly curls, she took a deep breath and set to cleaning up the breakfast dishes. She was halfway through peeling a batch of apples for a round of pies she *would not* let force her to clean the oven again when Aretha slipped through the swinging door, her limp lessened but still noticeable after all these months.

Whitney looked up from her task but refused to let her hands stop moving. "Can I get you anything?"

Aretha's eyes flickered with joy. "Not at all. I just wanted to give them a little alone time." She strolled to the adjacent counter and leaned a hip against it. "They'd make the most beautiful couple, don't you think?"

Choking back a cough of surprise, Whitney nodded. "Yes." Though she leaned toward the idea that with Daniel in it, any couple would look good. But that was information she had no business sharing with anyone, let alone his aunt.

"And they have so much in common." Aretha stole an apple slice from the growing pile in the big silver bowl and idly popped it into her mouth as she pulled a wooden stool around the island and gingerly lowered herself to it. "She graduated with honors in finance like him. And she lives in the city too."

Aretha's voice trailed off as though she was waiting for her to continue the conversation. Whitney split an apple in half, studying it more carefully than necessary. "Maybe they have mutual friends."

The older woman froze, a second slice halfway to her mouth. "Yes. Maybe they do. That would be perfect, don't you think?"

Unsure exactly what she was agreeing with, Whitney nodded.

"Imagine their life together. He's been so lonely, you know."

She knew no such thing, but Aretha didn't seem to notice.

"Lauren did—well, as Jack would say, she did a real number on his heart. He never let on about it. Kept it to himself and never even talked about it with his mom, but he must be lonely. I know I was. All those years before Jack came along. I don't want Daniel to have to wait as long as I did for happiness. And if anyone could make him smile again, it's certainly Ruby."

Aretha clapped her hands beneath her chin, her gaze darting toward the swinging door. When she spoke again, her voice was softer. "We'll have to work quickly."

We? Whitney could only mouth the word in Aretha's general direction as she sprinkled cinnamon and sugar and a dash of ginger over the bowl of apples.

"Of course, we. I can't possibly do it alone, and you're going to be here. They're both going to be here. But we only have four weeks left until Christmas." Aretha's voice rose with excitement until she covered her lips with her fingers and giggled. She shot a cautious glance at the door as though to make sure she hadn't been overheard.

Well, Whitney had heard everything Aretha had said, and she still wasn't sure what they were supposed to be doing.

Carefully stirring the pie filling until every apple was coated in a fine sheen, she waited for Aretha to continue. But the other woman was lost in her own musings, her eyes focused on the ceiling and a dreamy smile filling her face.

She wasn't sure she wanted to know Aretha's plan, but it was probably better to ask since Aretha had basically roped her into it. "What—exactly—do we need to do?"

"Why, get them to fall in love, my dear."

four

WHITNEY DROPPED her wooden spoon, and it clattered into the silver mixing bowl, catapulting a few apple pieces in an arch across the kitchen. They landed on the floor with a plop, but she couldn't tear her gaze away from Aretha's face.

She must have misheard. There was no way Aretha wanted her to help Daniel and Ruby fall in love.

"I'm sorry, get them to what?" she croaked.

Aretha smiled gently. "I want my nephew to have someone to lean on—someone who will take care of him when life doesn't go as planned." She shrugged and nodded toward her right foot. "I don't know what I would have done if I'd been alone when I broke this. Jack was . . . well, I hadn't known I could love him more than I already did. But I do. That man literally carried me all summer."

"You want Ruby to—to—to carry Daniel?"

With a laugh and a quick pat of her arm, Aretha shook her head. "Not literally. It's just that the Good Book says it's not good to be alone. I want him to have someone to help him when life is tough."

"What if he wants to be single?" Whitney was reasonably impressed with her own quick response, but Aretha responded even faster.

"He doesn't."

"How can you be so sure?"

A sadness veiled Aretha's face. "He was almost married. Three years ago. He was excited about their life together. Not exactly demonstrably. But I could tell. He wanted to build a life with her." Aretha shook off the gloom that cloaked her and replaced it with a smile. "So we're going to help him build a life with Ruby."

Whitney pressed a hand to her stomach as it bounced clean to the floor and then all the way up to her throat, where it promptly cut off her air. "A whole life together?" That seemed like more than falling in love.

"They are perfect for one another. Didn't we already decide? We just have to help them along a little bit."

"I can't—that is, I've never—I don't think I could be much help."

"Sure you can. We'll work together."

How could Whitney help when she'd never even been in love? Unless she counted from a distance. She'd been thoroughly smitten with her neighbors Roger Billings and Jeremy O'Connell in elementary school. And in high school there had been Josh Frank and Roger's older brother Randy. She'd even liked Jonah, the boy who'd sat behind her in church and pulled on each of her curls individually.

But not a single one of them had been interested in her. If she couldn't get a man to fall in love with her, how on earth could she make a man fall in love with Ruby?

Then again, Ruby wouldn't need much help. She was stylish. Educated. Decisive. She was everything Whitney was not.

A shot of envy burned through her chest at the memory of Ruby's perfect ponytail. Not a single hair even pretending to misbehave.

Whitney huffed at the frizzy curl that chose that moment to fall into her face.

Aretha stood up, pushing the stool away and favoring her injured foot. She leaned in close until her floral perfume nearly overtook the scent of the sweet cinnamon pie filling.

Whitney began shaking her head to answer her own question before she even asked it. "Do they even need help? Like you said, they're both good-looking and smart. Won't they figure it out on their own if it's meant to be?"

With a laugh of disbelief, Aretha somehow leaned closer. "Of course they need help. I love Daniel, but he won't make a move on his own. He's been too hurt."

"Maybe Ruby will."

Pursing her pale pink lips to the side, Aretha hummed. "Perhaps. But if she doesn't, we've missed our opportunity."

There flew that *we* again.

Aretha sighed and fell back onto the stool, making it scrape across the tiled floor. "Oh, I know it's probably none of my business, but you have to understand. He doesn't want to be alone. I know he doesn't. But if he waits too long . . . well, he's nearly thirty."

"Oh no, not thirty," Whitney singsonged, only a few years away from that dreaded birthday herself.

Aretha tsked but then laughed. "Very well, he's still young. But in this case he needs to listen to his elder." With a pointed look, she clearly implied Whitney needed to as well.

Whitney moved on to her pie crusts, wishing she could change this topic of conversation as easily. But it was clear

Aretha wasn't going to let go of the idea. "Why don't you ask Marie?"

"Ask me what?"

Whitney didn't even bother to turn around, her hands frozen in the flour jar, chin low, shoulders stooped. Marie didn't have time for Aretha's matchmaking shenanigans. She didn't even have time for her regular life right now.

And now she was going to assume that Whitney was volunteering her services to help set up a couple who probably didn't need it anyway. They wouldn't need four weeks to realize their connection—if there was one. She was betting on two. Maybe three, tops.

"We're going to set up Daniel and Ruby," Aretha whispered.

"Oh, really?" Marie said.

Without looking at her, Whitney couldn't tell if the other woman thought it was a great idea, so she risked a quick peek over her shoulder.

Marie was holding Jessie on one hip, her parka slung over the opposite arm.

"Are you going somewhere?" Whitney rushed around the kitchen island, reaching for the baby. Jessie immediately leaned over, snuggling against her shoulder.

"I've got to get Jack to the church for pageant practice. Can you watch Jessie for a couple hours? She'll go down for a nap in a little while."

"Sure." Whitney smoothed a hand over the little girl's dark curls, leaving a streak of white. An attempt to dust that off proved to only exacerbate the situation. Marie chuckled, kissed her youngest on the head, and called for her other two to meet her out back.

Which pretty much reiterated what Whitney had already

known. Marie didn't have space in her schedule to play matchmaker.

After the kids clomped down the back stairs and flew through the kitchen, stopping to give both Aretha and Whitney hugs, silence between the women hung heavy in the room.

Whitney knew what Aretha wanted. She also knew that her excuses weren't deterring the older woman.

When Aretha opened her mouth again, Whitney steeled herself against another onslaught.

"Your mother told me you're planning to attend culinary school in Charlottetown in the spring."

Whitney let out a soft sigh as she set Jessie on the floor with a pair of lids that she clanged together. "Yes. I'm hoping to. If I can earn enough at the Christmas markets to pay for tuition."

Aretha hummed an appreciative tune. "And if you don't earn enough?"

The question wasn't meant to be cruel. But it stabbed her just the same.

"I suppose . . ." She hadn't really let herself think about it. If she didn't make enough this year, she'd . . . well . . . she'd find a job. Maybe Caden's dad would hire her at the bakery. And she'd have to start the application process at the school all over again. She doubted they'd hold her spot. Not when there were so many other candidates ready, willing, and *able* to pay their tuition.

Whitney said none of that out loud, but Aretha seemed to know it anyway. "Perhaps I could make a donation to your tuition fund."

Her head spun for a moment, and she grasped the edge of the counter, sending a trickle of flour onto the babbling baby below.

"If you'll help me, I could see to it that whatever gap you have left at the end of the year is fully covered."

Whitney wheezed out a cough and stared unblinking at Aretha. It was too much. And it was everything she needed. "You can't be serious."

"Oh, I am. Extremely."

"But how could I be worth that much money? I don't know how to make people fall in love."

Aretha's coy smile slid into place. "There's no *make* about it. We just have to orchestrate the opportunity. They'll figure out the rest."

"But I don't have any ideas. I mean, what am I going to do? Hang up mistletoe and try to get them to kiss under it?"

With a cackle of delight, Aretha drew her into a warm hug. "See, you're already coming up with good ideas."

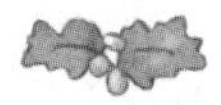

Daniel adjusted his glasses but still couldn't make sense of the numbers swimming before him on the computer screen.

Numbers never failed to add up, so it had to be his eyes. Or maybe Aretha's unique accounting system. He didn't remember it being quite so convoluted when she'd shown it to him all those summers ago. Or when he'd set her up with new software a few years before.

She clearly had a system. She just didn't always follow it. And there were far too many entries counted as sales for zero dollars. He rubbed his temples with his thumb and middle finger. Setting his laptop to the side, he stood and stretched his sore neck. Then his shoulders and arms. The stiff fabric of his button-up crackled as he moved, and he frowned at the cuffs tugging at his wrists.

He didn't need to wear his normal uniform. Not at the inn. And not for his aunt. But he hadn't brought anything else with him. Honestly, he didn't own much else, unless he counted the sweatshirt from uni that he wore to sleep. It had been washed so many times that it was softer than goose down. It also had a hole the size of Newfoundland under the arm.

Shrugging against the restrictive fabric, he strolled across the parlor, then pulled his knee up to his waist and held it for three seconds before taking another step and repeating the process.

"Will you grab that box, Jack?" Whitney's voice was almost as sweet as the scent of her pies, which insisted on floating up the stairs past the guest rooms and tempting him at all hours of the day and night.

The chatter of small children grew closer, and he scooped up his computer just before the littlest one arrived on all fours. She squealed, and it sounded happy, though he was not an expert on interpreting such things. Her siblings quickly followed, each carrying a cardboard box commensurate with their sizes.

"Mr. Danny!" The older girl's eyes lit up, and he tried not to cringe at the use of his nickname. "Are you going to dec-rate with us?"

"Daniel?"

He whipped his head up to see that Whitney had arrived, rolling a clear plastic bin in her wake.

"I'm sorry. I didn't know you were going to be in here. I assumed you'd . . ." She waved in the general direction of the bay across the street and the antiques store on the far side.

Maybe he should have gone with Aretha when she'd begged him to join her and Ruby in evaluating inventory, but he'd thought he would have a few quiet moments to review last year's books. That was looking like a pipe dream at the moment.

"Come on, kids. Let's let Mr. Daniel have some—"

"But you said we were going to dec-rate some more," Julia Mae said.

Whitney released her bin and squatted in front of her little charge. "We'll put up the decorations another time. Mr. Daniel has work to do."

Julia Mae stared up at him, her lower lip quivering dangerously and her huge blue eyes blinking against tears. Did someone teach girls how to do that, or did they come out of the womb knowing that move?

Whitney tugged on the little girl's hand and steered her toward the exit, but Little Jack hadn't moved, save for the frown that stretched across his face. The littlest one wasn't deterred, though. Daniel looked down as she crawled up to his foot and tugged on his slacks with chubby fists.

"She wants to be picked up," Jack mumbled.

"Oh, Jessie." Whitney raced to him and scooped up the little elf decked out in a red and white striped one-piece. Basically, a crawling candy cane.

At her fullest height, Whitney barely reached his shoulder. And at least some of that height had to be her hair. She'd attempted to restrain her curls with some kind of claw, but it was a losing battle, more than a few wisps falling into her face.

"I'm really sorry we interrupted you," she whispered, tiptoeing her way toward the door. "We'll come back later."

"You want to hang up more decorations?" He swung an arm wide to indicate the trimmed tree in front of the window.

Whitney's cheeks turned a sweet shade of pink as she glanced toward the ground. "There's still stockings to be hung, and the kids found another box of ornaments, so—"

"You can stay," he mumbled, not sure where the words had come from. He scowled at himself for inviting the extended interruption, shaking his head at his own foolishness. He'd have to make use of the desk in his room.

Whitney's lips opened, but before she could say anything, Julia Mae giggled with glee. "We're going to have the best time. Come on. Come on, Mr. Danny—"

"Mr. Daniel," Whitney corrected with an apologetic smile in his direction.

He nodded his appreciation.

"Mr. Daniel. That's what I said." Julia Mae placed her box on the steamer trunk turned coffee table and ripped off the lid to reveal an assortment of Christmas ornaments. It took her two seconds to empty the box across the tabletop, already oohing over the colorful figures.

Hugging his computer to his chest, Daniel shuffled around her, his escape mere steps away.

"Where're you goin'?"

Julia Mae's question made him freeze, and he pointed toward the stairs.

"But you have to help. Miss Whitney can't reach the top of the tree."

"Julia." Whitney's single word was sharp but not stinging. "Stop being bossy. He has important things to work on."

"Meemee Aretha said he's our guest. And guests don't work."

Whitney rolled her eyes. "Just leave him be, all right? As long as he has his computer, he's working."

Julia Mae ran up to him, nearly bumping into his knee

and staring straight up at him. "You can go put your pupe-tur down and then come right back."

"Julia Mae."

He didn't know if it was the exasperation in Whitney's voice or the innocence in Julia Mae's, but for some reason, he nodded. "All right. For a little while."

There was no telling who was more surprised—him or Whitney. But it was too late to back out now. Not with Julia Mae's smug smile as she handed him a fistful of ornaments and began directing him to open spots on the tree.

Little Jack soon joined him, hanging an assortment of homemade sleds and walnut-shell mangers until every branch was full. With each shift, a few needles sprinkled to the floor, the rich scent of pine filling the room.

When he turned after several minutes, he realized that Whitney had silently transformed the rest of the room. There was a string of garland over the wooden mantel. A red and green quilt across the back of the sofa. A wooden nativity scene set up on the corner table where he'd put his cup of coffee that morning. Those and a hundred tiny details made the room come alive with the spirit of the season.

At some point Whitney had put an old vinyl Christmas album on the wooden player in the corner. He caught himself humming along to carols so familiar that he could sing them in his dreams. And those were the only times he'd enjoyed them.

Until today.

The kids' laughter covered the music as the bigger ones threw sparkling tinsel across the branches they could reach. It didn't seem to bother them that the bottom half of the tree looked like a disco ball, the top half a deserted forest.

Imperfect and rudimentary. But it spoke to family. More specifically, to *this* family. A little messy, a lot of love.

"Dad says I can't stand up on chairs," Jack said, interrupting his thoughts.

Daniel stared at him for a long second before realizing that he was speaking to Whitney, who was shimmying up a step stool beneath the wooden entryway. The wide opening led directly into the main hallway and the dining room beyond, its dark wooden border now sporting more greenery with red ribbon wrapped loosely around it.

Toes pressing against the second step of the stool, Whitney stretched her arms far over her head, coming up just shy of the frame. With a harrumph, she took the last step. The stool leg slipped against the floor at that moment, and she wobbled precariously. Her arms flailed, seeking purchase, but she was too far from either side of the frame to find a hold as she let out an unrefined squeak.

Jogging three quick steps to her side, Daniel held out his hand, which she completely ignored for the support of his shoulder.

Her fingers were cold near his collar—even through his shirt—her grip surprisingly strong as she dug into him. Then she immediately let go, almost losing her balance again.

He hadn't touched a woman in years, but he grabbed her waist before he had time to think about it. Her curves were soft and smooth, warm. He'd only meant to steady her, but even when he was sure that she had regained her footing, he didn't let go.

And he couldn't stop staring at her. At the pink of her cheeks and the breathless laugh on her smooth lips.

"Thanks." She sighed. "Guess I should have had something to hold on to."

"That'd have been smart."

A flicker of a frown pinched her eyebrows together.

"What are you trying to do?"

She held up the loop of a wide gold ribbon, a bristly green ball bouncing from the other end. "Just trying to hang this."

Finally, he let go of her waist and took the ornament from her. "Let me."

The corner of her lip slipped between her teeth as she considered his request. After a long beat, she scampered down the steps.

"What's that?" Julia Mae asked.

Whitney shot him a guilty smile. "Mistletoe."

Daniel paused, one foot on the first step. Seriously? She had him hanging mistletoe.

"It's Marie's." Something about the way she said it made him think there was more to the story. He didn't press.

He only needed one step to reach the nail and easily hooked the trimming around it.

"See? I told you we needed you," Julia Mae chanted, dancing back to the tree, waving tinsel overhead.

"Oh, you've done it now," Whitney whispered at his elbow. "She'll be insufferable for the rest of the day."

He snorted. For the first time in longer than he could remember, he had to bite back a smile.

five

IT DIDN'T TAKE LONG for the rest of the house to follow the parlor, and within a few days every nook and cranny of the inn was decked out in its finest holiday trimmings. Banisters were beribboned and windowpanes had been frosted. Wreaths hung over doors, and even the swinging kitchen divider got a jingle bell.

"Maybe it'll protect Danny's nose," Big Jack had said, chuckling.

The tinsel on the Christmas tree had magically evened itself out, making the whole tree shimmer and shine as the afternoon sun poured through the front windows.

The trouble was that now Whitney had to find other ways to keep the children entertained. But that was tomorrow's problem. This fine Sunday morning she had only to deliver two plates of fluffy pancakes and apple sausage to the dining room before setting off for Summerside.

The Christmas market near the wharf would open in just two hours, and she couldn't afford to be late. The serious shoppers came early. And they spent their money quickly.

She'd already loaded up the coolers in her car with frozen pies that would save until Christmas Day. The fresh ones in the pink boxes on the kitchen counter boasted golden crusts and would need only fifteen minutes to warm up enough to melt a scoop of vanilla bean ice cream.

The scent of cinnamon and nutmeg hung in the air from her late-night baking dash. Or maybe that was the pancakes, announcing they were done. She scooped them from the skillet, slid three onto each plate, and snagged warm maple syrup from the microwave.

It wasn't fancy. No mint leaf garnishes or fanned strawberries. But it would be filling. And delicious.

"Coming through," she announced. She tucked two rolls of silverware under her arm, hoisted a plate in each hand, and spun through the door, the cheerful bell jingling at her back.

Daniel, Ruby, and Aretha were in their all-but-assigned seats at the four-top by the big window, their words low, voices intense.

"But they were included in the original inventory," Ruby said.

Aretha's lips pinched. "I may have forgotten to remove them from my system, but even if I did, that can't be the sole sticking point."

Whitney slid the plates in front of Daniel and Ruby, producing two wide smiles—Ruby's and Aretha's.

"Smells wonderful. As always," Aretha said.

After a glance at her wrist, where she hadn't worn a watch in a dozen years, Whitney nodded toward the kitchen. "There's more batter. You can help yourself, but I have to run."

Ruby chewed and quickly swallowed a prim bite. "Where are you off to?"

"The Summerside Christmas market."

"Outdoors?" Ruby looked like she'd bitten into a lemon. "But it's absolutely frigid."

"'S not so bad," Daniel said around a carefully portioned piece of sausage.

Whitney barely kept from asking him how he was so sure. As far as she knew, he'd been to precisely two locales since his arrival the week before. The inn and Aretha's store. He wasn't exactly exploring town and experiencing the chill. Maybe he guessed that since they'd only gotten a relatively light covering of snow this week, the weather was mild.

Well, he could assume that all he wanted from his spot on the couch in the parlor. Meanwhile, she had put on an extra layer of thermals that morning. Just in case.

"Have a lovely day," she said with a quick wave and a scoot toward the kitchen.

A hand around her wrist stopped her short. "Don't you think Ruby and Daniel would enjoy the market?" Aretha raised an eyebrow and shot her a pointed look. One that made her feel a tiny bit sick. "They're so festive and fun. And there are plenty of warm shops nearby to duck into if you get chilled."

"Oh?" Ruby sat up a little straighter. "I *should* probably do some Christmas shopping."

"Wonderful. It's decided then." Aretha let go of her wrist but shot her another look that seemed to convey Whitney was responsible for arranging a romantic rendezvous between the couple. "Ruby and Daniel will go with you."

Daniel had shoved exactly one-sixth of a pancake into his mouth at the precise moment his aunt announced his plans, so his "What?" was muted but still recognizable.

"That does sound fun. Don't you think, Daniel?" Ruby

didn't wait for him to respond, only glanced down at the silk blouse and straight wool trousers she was wearing. "I do need to put on warmer clothes, though."

Whitney looked again at her empty wrist, searching for words. "It starts in a couple hours."

Aretha smiled brightly. "Good, then you have plenty of time to get there. It's only forty minutes away."

Technically correct. But then there was traffic and setup, and what if her tent was cranky again? She twisted her hands into the loose apron ties at her middle.

With a gentle pat on her arm, Aretha said, "Don't fret. Daniel will help you set up your booth."

His eyes said he wasn't sure about any such thing. His eyes said he wasn't even sure how he'd gotten roped into going to the market.

She tried to give him her best smile as she nodded toward the kitchen. "I'm leaving in a few minutes. So . . ."

Ruby popped up on cue, leaving more than half her meal uneaten, and disappeared toward the front stairs without another word. Daniel did not. Stabbing the remaining four bites of his maple-covered breakfast, he grumbled at his plate. Then he scowled as he shoved the whole stack into his mouth.

Maybe she'd been wrong. Maybe his breakfast hadn't been as good as hers.

There wasn't time to dwell on it as she hustled into the kitchen, almost tripping on two pajamaed little ones. "Can we have some pancakes too?" Little Jack asked, his eyes as big as toonies.

"Yes, but . . . I have to . . . your mom can make them for you. The batter is all there."

Jack's shoulders deflated faster than a balloon. "Mom's still asleep."

With a quick glance at the clock on the stove, she sighed. She'd meant to leave fifteen minutes ago. She'd meant to get on the road before the sun was up, but the waves in the bay outside the kitchen window were already reflecting its morning greeting.

Perfect.

Julia Mae rubbed fists against her half-closed eyes as a yawn stretched her jaw. "Please. 'M hungry."

"Hey, you munchkins. Let Miss Whitney get on the road. It's her day off." Quick, muffled steps sounded from the office down the short back hall, and Seth poked his head into the kitchen. His hair had been styled by Serta, and the dark shadow across his jaw made him look a little scary—even to her.

His kids were not so deterred. "Daddy!" Julia Mae tackled his leg and then let him scoop her up and over his shoulder with a squeal that meant if Marie had been sleeping, she wasn't any longer.

"I'll make you pancakes. Now say goodbye to Miss Whitney."

"Bye, Miss Whitney," they chorused.

With one kid on his shoulder and the other hanging off his arm, Seth glanced at the stacks of pink boxes. "Can I help you with those?"

"Daniel will," Aretha announced as the two of them walked into the kitchen.

Whitney couldn't tell if Daniel's scowl was fresh or the same one he'd been wearing since his aunt had begun planning his day. "I'd appreciate it. Thank you."

Twenty minutes, Ruby's three coat changes, and "I just need one more scarf!" later, the trio was zipping down the highway toward Summerside. Whitney gripped the wheel a little harder than strictly necessary on clear pavement, but she had to focus on something other than Ruby's chatter.

"I can't believe this island. Is it always this beautiful? Imagine it with even more fresh snow. It will snow while I'm here, right? I mean, it must, this close to the water." In the passenger seat Ruby flipped up the collar of her Burberry coat and gave a full-body shiver. Whether it was from the cold or delight was anyone's guess. "I didn't realize there are so many farms. There's one. And that house has a red door too. Are red doors common here?" On and on she went.

Whitney wasn't sure why Ruby bothered asking questions. She never paused long enough to be answered. Ruby didn't seem to notice, though. She didn't ask questions for the answers, for the understanding. She asked to fill the void.

By that point, Whitney had almost forgotten what silence sounded like.

Fifteen minutes into the drive, she glanced into the rearview mirror. Daniel was folded into the back seat, his knees tucked under his chin, his gaze lost somewhere out the window. Three folding tables stretched across the collapsed seat beside him, and he curled in on himself as though he could become smaller.

When she checked again a few minutes later, his head was snapping back and forth with each passing pine tree—watchmen blocking homesteads and barnyards. Between the tall trunks, bursts of warmth from bright yellow sun rays broke through the misty morning.

Ruby commented on the lack of other cars on the road but didn't wait for someone to point out the crowded parking lot beside a white-steepled church.

They were nearly to Summerside when Whitney looked into the mirror again. This time Daniel was staring back at her. She jerked the steering wheel in surprise and earned a concerned chuckle from Ruby for her mistake.

With a quick movement, she righted the car and glanced up again. Daniel's blue eyes were bright, filled with something she couldn't quite name. It wasn't annoyance or exasperation, though she wouldn't blame him at this point. No one would.

It was softer than that. Richer. Lighter.

Whatever that look in his eye, it couldn't be humor. She hadn't seen the man crack a single smile in a week.

And he absolutely wasn't sharing it with her.

She forced her gaze to remain on the road the last few kilometers, watching for closed streets and detours. As they rounded the final turn, the street opened up before them, a wonderland of vibrant tents and bright wares bathed in the midmorning glow. Old brick buildings served as backdrops to the row of sellers, whisking them to bygone days.

"Oh, that's lovely," Ruby said. "Do you know where your spot is? How long will we be here? I have to go to every booth. Daniel, you'll help me carry my purchases, right? I can already tell I'll need at least one of everything."

True to her word, Ruby set off as soon as Whitney found a parking spot. "Come on, Daniel." She clapped her gloved hands together, prancing in place for several steps. Even then, she looked like she'd arrived for a photo shoot. Her plaid headband matched her designer coat, and the third scarf, the one she'd finally settled on—a red wool number—did complement the other pieces.

A chilly breeze tugged at Ruby's perfect ponytail, but she seemed oblivious to it. Meanwhile, Whitney wrestled with her own obnoxious mane.

"I'll catch up," Daniel grunted, unwinding his long limbs

and crawling from the back seat, stretching his neck from side to side.

"I'm sorry it was so cramped back there," Whitney said.

He shrugged it off and opened the trunk of her car before she could tell him she would handle setting up on her own. He unloaded the tables like they weighed the same as a pie. "Where to?"

"I'm space thirty-four. It should be right down there."

She followed him, pulling the fabric wagon that carried the first of several ice chests, display stands, tablecloths, and the pop-up tent.

Setting up the tent on her own was usually a comedy of errors. Especially when the booths on either side of her limited space were already in order. But Daniel pulled the tent from its canvas carrier, stared at its corners and hinges for five seconds, and opened it with a flourish.

"Something wrong?" Daniel asked. He must have noticed her staring at him.

"No, just . . . thank you. You really don't have to stick around. I'm sure there's something else you'd rather see here."

He lifted a shoulder. "I'm not much of a shopper."

"Which works out well since you're going to work for a retail company." She tried to keep a straight face, but a tiny smile broke through.

He paused, one hand on a table leg he was about to open, and sent her a questioning frown.

It was her turn to shrug. "Aretha may have mentioned it." Actually, Aretha had told every single person at church about her nephew's accomplishments in graduate school and the job he'd signed on to start with All Terrain, an outdoor adventure chain, after the New Year.

"Of course she did," he mumbled under his breath, but there was a hint of love in those words.

Aretha had been a surrogate aunt, grandmother, and mom to most of North Rustico over the years. But Daniel was truly family—and she wanted more than just a good job for him. She wanted true love and a happily ever after.

Whitney rubbed her stomach under her puffy parka as it twisted into a knot at the reminder that she was now at least partially responsible for making sure Daniel figured out his true love.

As they put the finishing touches on the booth—hanging the HOMEMADE HOLIDAY PIES banner between the tent's back legs—Whitney looked for Ruby, but the center aisle between the facing booths was already buzzing with eager shoppers. She'd stop by later. Surely.

That gave Whitney a little while to figure out what to say to encourage more than a professional relationship. At the moment, Daniel didn't seem too distraught at Ruby's absence.

Whitney slipped the glass cake cover over a plate of bite-size samples, but a glance at their golden edges and caramelized sugar tops made her steal just one. Lifting it to her mouth, she caught Daniel's gaze. He readjusted his rectangular black glasses, his eyes never leaving the stolen treat and its path toward her mouth.

"Do you want one?"

He nodded, so she raised the cover just enough. He pinched one too. And for a moment there was only sugar-fueled bliss. Sweet and tangy. Tart apples balancing the honeyed spices. Perfection in a single bite.

She licked her lips and forced herself not to reach for another as her first customer of the day strolled up. Like most farmers' markets, the day was marked with bursts of activity between long stretches of boredom.

But today Whitney wasn't bored. Not with Daniel peppering her with questions about why her sign said HOMEMADE HOLIDAY PIES instead of WHITNEY'S HOMEMADE PIES. Honestly, she hadn't given much thought to the branding. And why she waited for people to stop by before offering them a sample instead of going into the crowd and enticing them to the booth. That answer was easier to explain when there was usually only one person managing the booth, and she needed to stay close by.

But she had to admit that he had some good ideas. And he didn't tell her she was doing anything wrong. He simply asked why she'd chosen this or decided on that.

He may not have been much of a shopper, but his ideas had merit. No wonder he'd snapped up that CFO job.

About the time Whitney needed to replenish her pie supply from the cooler in her car, the wind picked up, carrying a distinct chill off the water. She shivered, and Daniel shoved his gloved hands into the pockets of his puffy jacket.

"I'll go get the pies," he offered. "It'll be good to warm up my muscles."

She pointed at her ears, which were covered by a toque and hopefully not as red as his. "I bet someone is selling a hand-knitted hat of some sort." She reached into her change purse and pulled out a bright green twenty. "It's my treat for your help today."

He waved her off. "They're my ears. Guess I better save them." He disappeared into the milling crowd.

She'd worked dozens of these markets on her own and had never felt lonely. Until that very minute. The feeling would pass, of course. But she wanted to shake it off immediately.

It was just that Daniel wasn't what she'd expected. He'd been surprising her since he arrived. And not just standing on the wrong side of her swinging door. The man was a contradiction down to his marrow. He didn't smile. He didn't laugh. But she knew in her heart that he loved his aunt with everything he had. He wouldn't be outside on a chilly island morning when he could be reading in front of a warm fire at the inn if it weren't for Aretha.

He didn't seem to be particularly friendly with anyone, yet Julia Mae had adopted him as her own. And Whitney hated to admit that when he'd helped the little girl reach a high branch on the tree, her heart had tripped over itself.

Daniel was clearly business savvy. He wouldn't have gotten the job that Aretha bragged about without the smarts to back it up. But he was also generous with that knowledge—offering suggestions for her small business, helping his aunt sell her store.

And accountants weren't supposed to be that handsome.

Whitney pressed her mittens to her face and shook her head to suppress a scream.

She needed to stop thinking about his face. The perfectly balanced angles of his jaw, his straight nose, and the little bit of scruff that had appeared that morning.

He was normally clean-shaven. Buttoned up. Literally. But his wavy hair had looked thoroughly disheveled since the breakfast table. Like he'd been running his fingers through it nonstop.

Which only made her want to run *her* fingers through it.

She had to stop.

He'd never look at her as anything more than Aretha's friend. More importantly, he wasn't for her. According to Aretha, he was for Ruby.

As though thinking of the other woman conjured her, Ruby shuffled into her booth, arms crossed and shoulders reaching toward her ears. Her whole body shivered as she stamped her booted feet. The paper bags hanging over her arm flapped in the wind. "It's so cold out here. I've really tried to make it, but it's far too much. Let's go back to the inn."

Whitney's insides twisted fiercely. "I can't just go. I have to be here all day." Besides, she'd only sold a third of the pies she'd brought.

Ruby's face crumpled, her perfect features suddenly looking less plastic and more human. "But I'm freezing."

Whitney bit back the strong desire to remind her that she'd swapped out her warmer coat for the name-brand one instead. "It goes with this outfit," Ruby had declared. And Whitney had whisked them down the road before Ruby could change her mind again.

Perhaps that had been a rash decision. Now they were stuck in Summerside. And it *was* cold, even with the evenly spaced patio heaters lining the aisle. But the cold hadn't bothered her when Daniel was around.

Not that she was going to think about that.

She was going to focus on the inn's guests, Aretha's happiness, and her own tuition.

"There's a cute shop down that way. Or there's a café at the end of the block. I'd be happy to buy you a cup of coffee, and you can stay inside until we're done here."

Ruby sighed. "How long will that be?"

Whitney glanced at the sun, which had already dropped behind the western buildings. "A few more hours. Maybe less."

"Hours? What am I supposed to do for hours?"

Now she had to entertain her too? "Do you have a book?"

Ruby's features pinched, and she shook her head with a long-suffering sigh. "Where's Daniel?"

Whitney rubbed at the strange tightness in her chest. "Getting more pies from the car."

"Fine. Send him down to the café when he's done. At least we can talk about the store while we wait." Ruby wandered off, her gait stiff and her shoulders hunched.

When Daniel returned several minutes later, Whitney let out a burst of laughter—right in the face of a customer. She quickly turned her back on Daniel and his new toque, apologized, and gave the young woman an extra sample. "Have a good day," she said, shoving a pink box into the woman's hands before dissolving into a fit of laughter.

"What are you wearing?" she said to Daniel, hugging her ribs to hold herself together.

"This?" He pressed a hand to his knit cap. "You like it?"

"It's ridiculous."

He shrugged. No smile. No chuckle. But that light was back in his eyes. The one she'd seen in her rearview mirror on the drive over. The one she'd first thought couldn't be a real, true sense of humor.

Now she knew she'd been wrong. It was. It had to be for him to wear that turkey hat, complete with little wings and roasted thighs sticking out over his ears.

That was twice in one day that he'd given her a peek at his humor. Maybe the grump was just a facade. So what was he trying to hide?

six

DANIEL HAD SOLD exactly zero pies in his life. It was an easy stat to remember. But he *had* aced more than a few retail courses. One of his professors had been keen to remind them that all the supply in the world meant nothing if you couldn't deliver it fast enough.

At least three women huddled at the back of the line winding out of Whitney's booth, their shoulders hunched against the wind and their gazes darting toward other stalls.

Whitney was tied up with a customer who wanted to sample every flavor. She was going to lose those sales.

Not on his watch.

"Who's next?" he called, raising a gloved finger to get their attention.

A middle-aged woman stepped toward him, then looked closely at his hat before snorting loudly. "Well, that's one way to stuff a bird, I suppose."

He shrugged, and the corner of his mouth tipped up briefly before his almost-smile disappeared. But the bubble in his chest didn't vanish quite so quickly. In fact, it had been there since he'd made Whitney laugh. Since he'd realized that had been his subconscious goal from the minute he saw the preposterous hat.

Her laughter started in her eyes, an undeniable glow. Then her whole face crinkled as though she was fighting to hold it in. The surprised note when it refused to be denied is what got him. It was sweet and rich and better than a sample of her pie because it echoed in his mind.

He could listen to her laughter for decades.

"Can I help you?" he asked the customer.

Whitney sidled up to his side, three frozen pies in her hands. "What are you doing?" she whispered through a smile.

"Don't worry. I'm a quick study." To his customer, he simply raised his eyebrows in question.

"An apple crumb and a boysenberry. Frozen."

He nodded, opened the cooler lids, and pulled out the pies. Each pink box was labeled with bold black letters in the lower right corner. Whitney's inventory system was impeccable. Better than Aretha's. Not that he was going to tell his aunt that. Besides, Aretha had a hundred times the products and a much larger variety.

Still, Whitney was doing well to manage the small business and bake all the supply on her own.

Perhaps she could use a hand in the kitchen.

He would have laughed at his own absurdity if he'd remembered how. There was no way he could be helpful in the kitchen. Shoot, he'd given up cooking for just himself and settled on takeout and frozen meals for . . . Had it really been three years?

No wonder he'd nearly stuffed a whole pancake in his mouth that morning. And the omelet yesterday. And the peach crepe the day before.

He'd had to force himself to carefully divide them into equal portions before devouring them. That was not a problem he had with limp broccoli and spongy beefsteak from the freezer section.

He frowned at Whitney's back, her voluminous curls bouncing over her shoulders as she moved from table to table, providing samples and filling orders. She glanced in his general direction, her dimple for the customers—he was an unintended beneficiary. Her smile still hit like a perfectly balanced ledger.

It had to be her cooking that made him feel like that.

Forcing his mind back to the woman waiting for the boxes in his hand, he pocketed her cash, passed along the pies, and waved to the next person.

With both of them taking sales, the line quickly disappeared, and finally Whitney leaned against a table with a sigh. "Thank you. I was going to lose a few of those if things didn't start moving."

"I figured."

"Well, thanks again."

"You're welcome."

Those two words were all it took to draw another smile—another chuckle—from her. "You've really saved me today, but I feel bad that the only shopping you've gotten to do is for that"—she waved a hand in the general direction of his face—"well, I can hardly call that a hat."

"Why not? It's covering my head and keeping my ears warm. Isn't that, by definition, a hat?"

Pressing her knitted gray mitten to her lips, she giggled. Her light brown eyes and bouncing shoulders telegraphed the merriment her hand had tried to muffle. "I'm serious."

"So am I," he said, leaning his hip against the table next to her. "It meets every criteria. This definitely qualifies as a hat."

"No." She pushed his shoulder playfully.

Even through the layers of stuffing, he could feel the warmth, the inherent familiarity of the contact. It stalled his mind for an instant.

"I meant, you should go see some of the other booths. Maybe there's someone selling outdoor wear."

"There is." The corner of his lips twitched.

Her eyebrows rose in a question.

"The guy who sold me this."

She burst out laughing, and he had to raise his voice to make himself heard. "And if you don't think I'm going to take this back to Toronto to show the All Terrain buyers, you're sorely mistaken. I know a thing or two about business."

The smile that showed off her slightly crooked teeth dimmed, then fully disappeared. "Ruby stopped by earlier."

"Hmm." He couldn't muster any more of a response.

"She was cold, so she said to tell you she's at the café at the end of the street. She said you should meet up with her and talk about the store."

He pursed his lips to the side and rubbed his hands together, the thought of spending the rest of the day with Ruby not particularly inviting. They would rehash the deal memo, and she'd remind him that Aretha hadn't been clear about the details. And then Ruby would talk some more. And she'd keep talking.

There'd be no laughter or crinkles around warm eyes. He wouldn't get to sneak another sample from beneath the glass dome or feel Whitney's warmth when he stood beside her.

"You can go," Whitney said. "I'll be fine here. And thanks to you, I only have a few dozen pies left to sell."

He looked in the direction of the parking lot and spotted

the yellow and black coffee sign hanging from the corner of the brick building. He'd walked by it on his way back from the car and had seen Ruby walking in. He'd also strategically turned his back toward her and hoped his turkey hat made him unrecognizable.

"I doubt they'd let me in with this on."

Her chuckle was dry and empty of actual humor. "I bet it comes off."

Finally, he shook his head. "I know what she wants to talk about, and I'm not particularly eager to have that conversation."

"Is it . . . does it have something to do with what you were talking about this morning at breakfast?"

He watched her closely, trying to figure out how she could pick up on such details. He hadn't even known she'd heard them at the inn.

"Aretha changed the subject pretty quick. It just seemed important."

"It is. Could be a deal-breaker."

"Oh." There was a sadness in the hushed sound. "Really?"

He nodded slowly.

"Do you want to—I mean, can you talk about it?"

"I imagine Aretha's told most of her friends by now." The negotiations should be confidential even though the agreements didn't explicitly state that, but he knew the island worked on a different system. If Aretha was right, handshakes and verbal contracts weren't unusual among townsfolk.

But Ruby wasn't a local. And she certainly didn't work for an island company.

Maybe he could get Whitney's input without actually revealing any of the details. And he wanted her input. As a small business owner. As an islander. As a friend to many of the women of North Rustico. He wanted to know where her thoughts went, what she'd do if put in a similar position.

Wading in slowly, he said, "Between you and me?"

She nodded.

"This is entirely hypothetical."

"All right."

"Say you were working with a storefront that agreed to sell your pies for a certain price and give you a portion of the profit."

"You mean like what Aretha does with quilts and things? My mom bought one from her last year. Margie Giffins made it to look like the island's intersecting red roads. It's beautiful."

He rolled his eyes as the hypothetical went right out the window. Everyone knew everyone's business on the North Shore.

"Sorry." She ducked her head. "Go on."

"How would you feel if the store owner sold their shop—and your consignment agreement with it?"

"Would I still get paid?"

"Some."

Squinting at him, she crossed her arms and tilted her chin up. "Not what I had agreed to?"

"Probably not."

She pushed herself off the edge of the table and pressed her fists to her hips, her gaze turning to fire—amber flames replacing the warm brown depths. "You can't cheat those women out of what they're owed. They spend dozens of hours on those quilts, hundreds of dollars."

"Whoa. Whoa. Whoa." He stepped closer to Whitney, forcing her to tilt her head all the way back to maintain eye contact.

She didn't back down, though. In fact, she shuffled toward him, closing the gap and staring him down.

"I'm not cheating anyone out of anything. And neither is Aretha. You know her better than that."

"Right. Well, don't." Her voice dropped in pitch. "It's not right. Especially at this time of year."

Like July would make the situation any more palatable.

"Can't you just give them back their quilts?"

"Hypothetically"—he nodded with each syllable—"yes. That's what I'd like to do. But R & R wants those to remain in inventory."

Her eyes narrowed, exactly as his had the first time he'd heard the proposition. But her question was different. "R & R?"

"Rogen & Reynolds. The conglomerate that Ruby works for."

"Okay. So, why don't they just buy them from the makers?"

He shook his head. "They want all of the inventory to stay with the store." Ducking his chin, he conceded, "And Aretha may have forgotten to remove those from the initial documents she sent over."

"But they have to understand . . ." Her voice trailed off as she stared in the direction of her car, though the view was dominated by the big gray theater and colorful shops on the shore.

The rub was, the numbers made sense—even without the quilts. The store was profitable and had been for years. Aretha's agreement with the quilters was a gift to the community. Not a moneymaker for her.

"Ruby said she'd go back to her boss about it, but the whole thing could fall apart."

"And then she'd leave . . ." Whitney's rounded eyebrows

flattened as they pinched together, forming three little lines above her nose, wrinkling her otherwise pristine skin.

"I guess." He would too. Though she probably didn't care about that.

"You should go talk with her. Get it worked out."

"I will. But not today. Not until I figure out how to convince her."

"Oh, but that's the easy part." Whitney promptly turned her back on him and straightened several pies on display.

He stared at the back of her shoulders for several long seconds, finally clearing his throat.

She turned around with raised eyebrows.

"The easy part? Care to expound?"

She chuckled. "I thought it was obvious," she said just as four young women approached the booth, their cheeks rosy from the weather and their arms laden with shopping bags. Instead of answering his question, Whitney introduced herself to the shoppers, who were full of questions about her homemade pies. How long did it take to make them? Did she have a secret recipe? Would their moms realize they hadn't made the pies themselves?

The last question made Whitney throw back her head and laugh, all of her abundant curls dancing with delight, her eyes lit from within.

If a picture was worth a thousand words, the sight of Whitney laughing could fill a dictionary. She was joy personified. Warmth in motion.

She cupped the elbow of the closest shopper and leaned in with a conspiratorial whisper. "I promise it'll be our little secret. Your mom will never guess."

The girls cackled, handed over their cash, and walked away with stacks of pink boxes. And very broad smiles.

When they were on their own again, Daniel crossed his arms and tried to analyze what made Whitney so magical.

She caught him looking and playfully swatted his arm. "What are you staring at?"

"Just wondering . . ." He bit his tongue, not wanting to admit exactly what he'd been thinking. "Just wondering if you're going to tell me the obvious solution to the *hypothetical* situation with Aretha's store."

"Sure. I mean, it's just a suggestion, but—here's the thing. Everyone wants the store to succeed. Aretha, the new buyers, the community. Everyone. But if the new buyers don't give Aretha or the quilters—"

"Hypothetically."

She laughed. "Yes, whoever the craftswomen are. If the buyers don't treat everyone fairly, the store will suffer. This community won't stand for it."

"But most of the business comes during tourist season. Those customers won't know what R & R did or didn't do."

Whitney sniffed, her lips twitching to the side. "And who do you think points customers to the antiques store? Every other tourist shop in town."

That made sense. It made a lot of sense.

Whitney put her hands on her hips. It probably didn't have the effect she was going for—what with her puffy jacket making her twice as round as usual. But he still got the point that he was supposed to pay attention.

"Store owners support local craftspeople. And each other. If they get even a whiff that the new owners of Aretha's store didn't treat one of their own fairly, you better believe they'll see it shut down. They'd rather not have an antiques store in town than have one that takes advantage of people." Whitney crossed her arms over her chest. "So you'll talk with Ruby?"

He nodded. He'd always planned to. But now, maybe he had something she'd hear.

"Soon?"

Before he could agree, they were swamped by another rush, this one mostly men looking for the pie samples they'd heard about. And then claiming their wives didn't want to have to bake Christmas treats this year. Daniel wasn't quite sure he believed them, but he couldn't argue with the colorful bills they shoved in his direction.

Whitney had only three pies left as the temperatures dipped and the crowds that had filled the street all afternoon turned thin. Sitting down on the cooler lid, Daniel pulled his coat closed beneath his chin and breathed into his hands. Like an idiot.

His warm breath didn't have a chance of reaching his freezing fingers. Not through his gloves anyway.

Whitney offered him a pitying smile. Sliding onto the seat beside him, she pulled a blanket from the wagon and flopped it over their laps, her hands nimble—clearly not suffering from the same frostbite his were.

"We don't have to stay much longer."

He nodded, the turkey legs bouncing over his ears.

Whitney's gaze darted to his hat, and her whole face crinkled as she seemed to hold in her laughter. Just remembering her reaction the first time she'd seen it was enough to almost elicit a smile of his own. Almost.

They sat in companionable silence for ten minutes or so—interrupted only by Whitney's occasional greetings to passersby. One minute the sun wrapped its last rays of warmth around them. The next it disappeared beneath the horizon, and the street went almost black. For the shortest moment.

Like in a movie, Christmas lights split the darkness. Some

twinkled gently like stars. Others zipped around tent poles, chasing an unseen goal. Rows upon rows of open Edison bulbs strung between the buildings over the center aisle woke up slowly, glowing first orange and then finally popping to bright white.

Within seconds the scene that had been loud fell silent, every eye looking up, every face luminous with wonder.

Beside him, Whitney held her breath, as though simply inhaling might disturb the magic. When she finally sighed, she lifted her face toward the sky and shut her eyes. "Don't you love it when you close your eyes but can still see the light?"

For the first time all day, he frowned in earnest. Not because he disagreed with her but because he wasn't sure he'd ever once had that thought. He knew the feeling, of course. He'd spent far too many summers in Aretha's backyard under the island's brilliant sun not to.

But had he ever appreciated it?

Unlike Ruby's questions, he thought Whitney's deserved an answer. He just wasn't sure what it was.

"I guess so."

"You guess so?" She shook her head hard and peeked at him out of the corner of her eye. "Look at the lights."

He didn't. He was too busy staring at the glow beside him.

"Loo-ook," she said again, imitating Julia Mae's emphatic direction.

He complied, picking one antique bulb at the end of a string, its light illuminating the orange bricks behind it.

"Now close your eyes." She released a little whispered sigh. "I love that moment where the bulb disappears but the filament burns even brighter. It's like what's real, what's most true, remains."

Strange. She was much the same. Even when she was gone,

her warmth remained. Even when her smile disappeared, her light shone around her.

He'd never met anyone like her. And he wanted to know all the parts of her.

He had no business entertaining such thoughts about a woman he'd met only a week before—one he'd never see again after Christmas.

But there they were, and he couldn't seem to let them go.

seven

"I'LL LEAVE YOU kids to it, then."

Daniel looked up from the inventory book in his hands and frowned at his aunt. There was something knowing in Aretha's tone. At least, that's what it sounded like to him. Then again, he'd never understood women his own age. Why should it be different with older women?

But he couldn't shake the idea that she was implying *something*. Even if he didn't know what it was.

After nodding toward Aretha, he looked back at Ruby, who was holding up a globe at eye level. Her focus intent on the antique, she said only, "See you tonight."

Aretha waved and disappeared, closing the door behind her, leaving him and Ruby alone. With about three hundred pieces that needed to be inventoried and eventually moved to the front of the store and sold. But for now, newly acquired pieces filled the storeroom. The shelves that lined each wall were packed with dishes, clocks, and sundry knickknacks. And the open cement floor was a maze of furniture and larger items, all with a distinct island charm.

Actually, the storeroom didn't look much different from the front of the store. Save a thick layer of dust. Aretha kept her items for sale neatly dusted, and if she had invested in Swiffer years ago, she could have retired before she broke her foot. Before she left him alone with Ruby, inferring whatever it was she had been inferring.

He scowled. It didn't matter what Aretha thought they'd be up to alone in the room. Daniel knew what needed to be done. And thanks to Whitney, he knew how to do it.

"Ruby."

She set the globe down, satisfied with its condition, and turned to a lantern that had once sat in the top of a lighthouse. "This is enormous. So much bigger than they look from a distance. Or out at sea, I guess. Must have been for a really big lighthouse."

"Probably not. Just an older one." The lantern was no taller than his waist, but the newer lights didn't need to be bigger. They just used better magnification.

"Huh." Ruby cocked her head and glared at the glass panels that had once extended the light over the water. "Well, it seems plenty big to me. I mean, any bigger and it would just take over a whole room."

"Good thing they weren't made to go inside homes then."

Ruby's gaze snapped to him, her blue eyes sparking with something that made him want to back up slowly and then run very, very quickly. His words may have come out a bit sharper than he'd intended.

That probably wasn't the way to start a conversation in which he was going to ask for a favor. Well, it wasn't strictly a favor. He just needed her on his side.

A side that probably wouldn't look very appealing from where she stood.

He opened his mouth to say something. Only he didn't know how to say it. He'd spoken the truth before, but women didn't always like the truth. At least in his experience.

After several long seconds of silence, Ruby huffed and turned her back to him. "Mark it as acceptable." Whipping around to the rolltop desk beside her, she shoved the sleeves of her sleek blue sweater to her elbows and opened drawers.

Daniel did as she ordered, putting a black check mark next to the line item.

Time to get them back on track. He just needed to . . . how had Whitney put it?

The corner of his mouth pinched upward of its own accord at the mere thought of the way Whitney's frenzy of hair had glowed beneath the market lights the day before. She'd almost had a halo, and he let his mind wander for a moment, picturing angels with wild honey-colored curls.

Whitney would know what to say to smooth over his last faux pas too. But she was probably back in the inn's kitchen, rebuilding her supply of pies for the next fair, flour on her apron and hair frizzy about her face.

He'd rather be there helping her. Or, more likely, getting in her way.

Clearing his throat, he forced his face to a neutral expression. Not that Ruby was looking at him. She was too busy rolling the desk's top up and down. It stuck for a second but then slid along smoothly.

"Aretha acquires quality pieces, eh?" he said.

Ruby shot a glance in his direction. "She does have a good eye."

Okay, this was good. Progress, maybe. At least she wasn't glaring at him anymore like he'd insulted her. Though he still wasn't entirely sure he had the first time.

Pointing to a row of blue and red leather-bound books on a shelf, Ruby said, "We'll keep these too."

He added a check mark. "According to her records, Aretha paid a fair market price for the first editions."

"I'm sure."

With Ruby's back turned, he took a sustaining breath and blurted out the words that had been looking for an opening. "Shouldn't the quilters get fair market value for their products too?"

She froze, her neck like steel. Even the hair in her ponytail got the message and refused to be budged by the breeze from the ceiling fan that moved heated air through the otherwise stale room. Slowly she turned toward him, her eyes narrowed. "We've had a lot of success with local artisans in other markets."

"Sure. And you can here too. Why not just buy the quilts from the quilters and keep the inventory?"

Ruby set down the gilded picture frame she'd been holding and dabbed the back of her wrist against her forehead. He didn't point out the stripe of dust across the stomach of her sweater.

"Aretha included them in the original inventory," she said, sounding like she'd already tired of this discussion.

"But the store is a fair price without the quilts."

She inclined her chin in a gesture that said she'd heard him—not that she agreed with him. "The offer was for everything on the original list with adjustments to be made for any inventory deemed inadequate." With a graceful sweep of her arm, she indicated the items in the storeroom and exactly what they were doing.

Daniel clapped his hand to the back of his neck, his chin falling to his chest. "And you've decided that twenty-five quilts—what amounts to about ten grand—is worth losing the whole acquisition?"

Ruby shook her head. "You know that Aretha won't let this opportunity pass. She hasn't had any other offers for a reason."

Tapping his pen against the open inventory book, he frowned. True enough, there wasn't a crowd of buyers fighting to buy a small store like this. But it didn't mean Aretha was desperate.

"Aretha can do whatever she wants to with the money we're paying her." Ruby picked up some sort of chicken-shaped knickknack and scowled at it. "If she wants to pay for the quilts out of that, she absolutely can."

"But that would be shortchanging her." Daniel wanted to add that this money was her pension. It would allow her and Jack to travel, to treat their grandkids. But Ruby wasn't interested in sentiment.

She sighed. "No one is losing here. The amount we've proposed is fair. However Aretha chooses to spend it."

"But at what cost? Either you're taking advantage of Aretha or the local artists. Do you think that's going to earn you any favors with the rest of the community?"

"All 607 of the local residents?" She snorted dismissively and shook her head. "Which probably includes Marie's baby. And I doubt she's doing much shopping here. We're counting on the tourists."

"Yes . . ." He dragged the word out and then took a deep breath, summoning his best impression of Whitney. "But who do you think points people to this store? This community recommends each other. With every cone bought at the ice cream shop on the boardwalk. Every kayak that's rented. Every chocolate croissant from the bakery. Those business owners point customers here."

Her eyes narrowed, and he jumped to continue.

"They won't if you've shorted their moms and grandmas. They'll warn people away."

Dusting her hands at her waist, she frowned. He could practically see the numbers crunching behind her eyes. "I'll look into it."

Whitney nearly dropped her pie when the inn's back door slammed and Aretha pranced into the kitchen through the mudroom. She practically twirled as she unwound the red scarf from her neck.

"Oh, it's such a lovely day to fall in love, don't you think?" Aretha sighed.

"Um . . ." Whitney closed the oven and set the timer. "I suppose . . ."

Plopping onto one of the stools and propping her elbows against the island's white-tiled countertop, Aretha rested her chin on her fists.

Whitney couldn't help but laugh at the older woman's antics. "Been doing a little matchmaking, have you?"

"I just left Daniel and Ruby together for a whole afternoon, practically locked in the storeroom."

Her stomach did an unpleasant flip, and she stumbled to understand why. "You, um, you locked them in there?"

"Of course not. But I may have suggested that we really need to get the inventory onto the floor, so they had better finish up in there today." Unbuttoning her coat, Aretha giggled like a woman half her age. Check that. A quarter of her age. Her gray curls bounced, and her pale eyes shone with pure delight. "It was just a little bit of encouragement, really."

"So, your plan is . . ." Whitney didn't quite know what she wanted to ask, so her voice trailed off.

"Our plan, dear." Aretha winked. "*Our* plan."

Whitney nearly swallowed her tongue. This certainly hadn't been her idea. Not a week ago when Aretha had hatched it, and certainly not now that Daniel had told her about Ruby's disregard for the quilters.

Hypothetically.

Filling the sink with sudsy water, she wrinkled her nose as she tried to ask what she couldn't seem to. "The plan is—that is, do you really think—I mean—" She picked up a slippery ceramic bowl, which splashed into the dishwater. When she glanced over her shoulder with an apologetic smile, Aretha was staring at her, a concerned frown wrinkling her white eyebrows.

"Honey?"

Picking up the bowl with a firmer grip, Whitney took a deep breath. "Do you think Ruby and Daniel are a good fit?"

An airy laugh tittered through the room. "Is that what's bothering you?"

Whitney wanted to nod, but there was still something gnawing at her insides, hungry for the whole truth.

Ruby wasn't good enough for Daniel.

There. That was it. The crux of the issue. Ruby was trying to take advantage of Aretha and the town's quilters and . . . well, the situation. And didn't Daniel deserve someone with more integrity? Surely Aretha wanted the very best for her nephew.

Aretha stood and poured herself a cup of coffee from the endless pot on the counter. "They're perfect together. He's a serious young man and needs someone equally as driven."

Or maybe he needed someone who could drive away his perpetual scowl.

Not that Whitney had any idea how to do that. But there had to be someone who could make him smile. Maybe it was Ruby.

She pictured the professional's tight expression, prim posture, and chattering ways.

Probably not.

Ruby would never laugh at his turkey hat. And Whitney was pretty sure a chuckle had been what he was going for. Even if he hadn't spared one himself.

"He needs someone who can move in the same circles at work." Taking a slow sip of her coffee, Aretha seemed to give herself a mental nod of affirmation. "Ruby can host dinner parties and talk business with his new colleagues. She can advise him and encourage him."

She certainly looked the part with her sleek hair and tailored outfits. Ruby would fit right in with the other businesspeople.

The berry pie filling Whitney had sampled earlier turned suddenly sour in her stomach. She would never fit into Daniel's life.

Not that she wanted to. Or had any business even pondering such a thought. It was a nonissue, a never-would-be. She barely even knew the guy.

Moreover, she had her own plans that did not involve Daniel Franklin. And she was mostly sure she wanted to pursue them. If only to show her mom and dad that she could. That she *would*.

"Besides, I'm not sure he knows what he needs," Aretha said. "Not after Lauren."

Right. Lauren. His . . . someone from the past. Something that had ended badly.

She wanted to ask what had happened, if Lauren was the reason for the sadness in his eyes. But she had no business poking into that. Her dad would say that was how gossip started—asking questions about someone who wasn't there. Questions that didn't need to be asked. Questions that couldn't help.

She wouldn't be digging in for Daniel's sake but to slake her own curiosity. So she bit back her queries and rinsed her dishes until Aretha spoke again.

"He needs someone stable. Not someone flighty or . . ."

Whitney glanced over her shoulder to find Aretha staring dreamily off into space, probably completely oblivious to the jab of her words.

Even if Aretha hadn't meant it that way, Whitney could practically hear the end of that sentence ringing out. After all, her dad had reminded her regularly. "Quit being so flaky, Whitney. Pick something and stick with it."

Her stomach twisted again.

Well, she had. Culinary school. That was her plan. Until . . .

No. There was no *until*. There was nothing better coming around the bend. There was only culinary school. A job as a pastry chef. Her desserts delighting foodies across the island.

The end. Decision made.

This wasn't like nursing school at UPEI. It wasn't like the expensive fiddle she'd put down after a month. Or the high school theater production she'd dropped out of after two weeks.

Culinary school was her future.

Aretha sighed, pulling Whitney back into their conversation. "He needs someone like Ruby in his life."

"But how do you know Ruby is the right one? Maybe there's someone—I don't know—better for him." Someone who wasn't trying to take advantage of their community.

A slow grin settled across Aretha's wrinkled face. "Perhaps she needs someone like Daniel." With a wink she added, "I think she'll prove herself yet."

Aretha had to be talking about the negotiations, and surely she knew more about what was being discussed in hushed conversations over the breakfast table.

Whitney tried to shake off the unease, but the knot in her stomach remained. "I'm just not sure they're . . . suited for each other."

Aretha's features turned thoughtful, her face wrinkling more than usual as she plucked at the skin below her chin. Finally she asked, "Do you want out of our deal?"

"No!" Whitney blurted out, but a brick lodged in her throat as soon as she said it. Because she did want to back out of their agreement. Actually, she'd never wanted to be part of it in the first place.

The trouble was that Aretha's offer to chip in for school was her only safety net. And, if she was honest, it was her only real hope of making tuition for the next term. Her pies had been selling, but the profit margins were so low that she'd have to sell a thousand more before Christmas to hold her place at the school.

Yet Aretha's help came with strings.

The strings weren't the problem. They'd been on the table since the start. The problem was how easily Whitney had been swayed by them. How she was so quickly convinced with a brief reminder of the money.

She dropped her chin to her chest and took in a tight breath. "No. I'm not going to back out. I just want to make sure we don't waste our time."

"Trust me." Aretha chuckled. "I set up Marie and Seth. Caden and Adam too. And I knew Natalie and Justin were meant to be from the time they were kids. I see the same something special between Daniel and Ruby."

eight

DANIEL FROWNED as he scrolled slowly through yet another spreadsheet. This was the seventh one his aunt had sent him this week. And there were another ten or twelve to go—if she was to be trusted.

He knew her to be a capable bookkeeper, except for her penchant for marking items sold at zero dollars. If no money exchanged hands, it wasn't a sale. But he couldn't be sure how many of the null figures were broken items. Or maybe they were gifts.

That was how Aretha had always worked. If someone saw something they liked and couldn't afford, she'd give it to them. If a child wanted a unique gift for Mother's Day, Aretha made sure they had it.

She'd been like that as long as he'd known her.

But he couldn't pass off an incomplete log with a flimsy excuse that that was just the way Aretha did things. So he tapped a few quick notes into the spreadsheet—reminders to follow up with her.

Then, with brisk keystrokes, he produced a graph of

monthly earnings. They were on a steady incline. Nothing that would make headlines, but the trajectory was definitely positive.

And her outgoing expenses hadn't increased much over the years. Rent on the property hadn't gone up in about a dozen years, and sales had more than outpaced the slow rise in heating and cooling costs.

The store was a solid investment. It wasn't going to make anyone rich, but it was a community staple. It would remain that way, so long as Ruby convinced her bosses to back down. She had to.

Before he could begin imagining what that conversation would be like, light footfalls skipped down the hallway outside the parlor. Craning his neck, he tried to find the source of them, but he was still alone in the cozy room. Just him, the oversized Christmas tree, and that ridiculous ball of mistletoe.

He scowled at its bright red and gold bows for no reason other than that it had the gall to be so merry. The tree was pretty joyful too, all glittery and glowing in the afternoon sun. Sure, the kids probably loved it, but he hadn't been a kid in a long time. And the last time he'd had a merry Christmas . . .

Those Christmas memories were all stained now.

His eyebrows pinched together, and he punched the keys on his laptop harder than necessary.

Out of the corner of his eye, he thought he saw some movement in the doorway, but then it was gone. A few seconds later, the same thing.

Maybe he'd been staring at the screen too long. There was no use in pushing through to finish this project. Aretha had made him promise he'd stay for Christmas. At least. And Ruby had said she would talk with her boss early the next week.

Might as well have something to do to fill the time. The

Lord knew he wasn't going to spend it on the trappings of the season.

Lifting his glasses and rubbing his eyes with the heels of his hands, he leaned his head on the back of the sofa. The ceiling was covered in an intricate pattern—something that was probably popular on those DIY design shows—so he let his gaze wander through its curves and hollows as he closed his laptop.

Immediately the sprite appeared around the far arm of the cozy blue sofa, her blue eyes enormous and her dark curls bouncing with each skipped step. "Miss Whitney says I can't bother you while you're working. You're done now."

Her pronouncement held so much conviction that he almost believed it.

Little Julia Mae held out a book that was half as big as she was, and when he didn't immediately take it, she shoved it into his hands. "You can read to me now."

Daniel couldn't keep in the snort that her statement elicited. "Oh, really?" He flipped the hardcover book right side up. The collected stories of Winnie-the-Pooh. Classic.

She nodded firmly before putting her hand on his knee and crawling up beside him. She wedged herself into the space by his hip and leaned over to look at the book.

It was strange, that feeling of her tiny hand on his arm, so trusting, her little fingers squeezing the stiff sleeve of his button-up.

Most people took one look at him and kept their distance. It wasn't like he didn't have *any* friends. But they were from before. They knew. They understood. And they expected nothing but what they got.

Julia Mae was something completely different. She didn't know about his past. And she didn't seem to care.

Oh, to be a child again.

"You can start with the second story. I don't like the first one." Her little nose wrinkled up at the mere mention of the disliked tale, making a few of her freckles disappear.

"Why not?" The question surprised even him.

"Pooh gets stuck, and I got stuck one time. In the cupboard in the kitchen." Long black lashes lowered over her eyes, and her lips pursed to the side as though she was trying not to remember the memory. "I was scared. Papa Jack saved me, though."

"I'm glad to hear he saved you." Taking another look at the book in his hands, he shook his head. "Maybe you should ask him to read to you."

She tilted her head, peering intently at him. "But I asked you."

"I should get back to work."

"But you're taking a break. You closed your screen. I waited until you were done." Her lower lip trembled in the middle, her eyes turning glassy.

His gut twisted sharply. Flipping open the book, he sighed. "The second story?"

Julia Mae's bow-shaped lips immediately formed a bright smile that displayed her baby teeth, any hint of tears vanishing.

Little faker.

Daniel began reading the story as Julia Mae leaned over his arm. He traced his finger beneath each line as he spoke, a habit he'd picked up in grad school to help him memorize information. This wasn't so academic, but before he could pull his finger back, she put her little hand on top of his. He glanced over to see her mouthing each of the words as they pointed to it.

The story of Pooh bear and his friends quickly came to an end, punctuated by Julia Mae's contented sigh. She leaned back into the sofa, folding her interlaced fingers against her belly like a man who'd eaten too much and was in search of a good nap.

"You're kind of like Eeyore, aren't you? Sad sometimes."

She said it with no guile, no agenda. Only the truth. Kids had a way of doing that, cutting to the quick.

But he didn't like thinking of himself like that. He wasn't sad. Exactly.

He couldn't bite back his scowl fast enough, and her eyebrows rose, her pert little nose wrinkling. "You shouldn't be sad, you know. It's almost Christmas. And no one's sad at Christmas." Julia Mae hopped to her knees and bounced on the cushion. "There's presents and pie—Miss Whitney makes the best pie. And Mama is always singing Christmas songs. And on Christmas Eve"—her voice dropped in hushed wonder—"we get to light candles."

"Candles, eh?" He matched the pitch of his voice to hers.

She nodded vigorously. "And Jack is going to be in the pageant this year. He's the star."

Daniel wasn't sure if that meant Jack was the star of the show or the literal star of Bethlehem. But there was no time to ask for clarification as Julia Mae chattered on, stopping only when her name rang through the inn.

"Julia Mae!" Pounding footsteps in the hallway behind him stopped as Whitney flung herself into the room. Honey-colored curls had escaped her ponytail, framing her face and the trail of flour down her cheek. "There you are." She sighed. Only then did she seem to notice him, a guilty grin breaking out as she wiped her hands on the flowers of her apron. "I'm sorry," she said. Then to Julia Mae, "I told you I'd read to you after I put the pies in the oven."

"But Mr. Daniel wanted to read to me."

He nearly choked, holding back a snort at her brazen lie.

Whitney wasn't buying it. Crossing her arms over her chest, she stared down her nose at her young charge. "Would you like to take a nap like Jessie?"

Julia Mae scrambled from the couch and yanked the book from his grip. "Thanks," she whispered before darting toward her nanny. With one apologetic look at Whitney, she disappeared into the hallway.

"I'm sorry about that." Whitney's smile returned, gentle and soothing—all hint of the reprimand she'd had for Julia Mae gone. "We'll try not to interrupt you again."

"It . . ." His voice trailed off as he tried to find the words. He ended up with a muttered "No problem."

The truth rang somewhere deep inside him. It had been fun.

Her gaze darted around the otherwise empty room. "No Ruby today?"

He shrugged. "We finished the inventory, and she had some video calls with the home office. I was just going over some more of the financials."

Whitney glanced over her shoulder toward the kitchen. "If you're not busy, we're going to walk over to the church in a bit and pick up Little Jack from pageant rehearsal and then go look at Christmas lights."

His gaze darted toward the window. It couldn't possibly be late enough, but the afternoon sun had already dipped low in the sky. It wouldn't be long before the twinkling lights shone at their brightest.

"Would you like to come with us?"

Daniel bit back his immediate response, forcing his face to remain impassive.

Whitney swallowed quickly. "And you should invite Ruby to come too."

"Invite me where?" Ruby swished into the parlor, her hair, makeup, and crisp red shirt all pristine. Not a wrinkle in sight.

Daniel almost rolled his eyes as he noted that she was wearing creased black dress pants—and a belt too. Nearly everyone he knew dressed for video calls from the waist up. Business on top, party on the bottom. Or at least relaxed on the bottom.

He glanced at his own khaki pants and tugged at the cuffs of his button-up. He hadn't even had a meeting today, unless you considered Julia Mae. And she couldn't have cared less what he was wearing, so long as he kept reading.

"The kids and I are going to look at the Christmas lights when Seth gets home. Mr. Huntington does a huge display every year." Whitney's eyes lit up. "Would you like to go with us?"

Ruby ran a hand over her ponytail, her features turning a bit grim. "Are you going to drive?"

Whitney looked confused. "We'll walk. It's just a few blocks."

"But . . ." Ruby looked at him as if asking for help. But Daniel didn't have any to offer.

"I'll go," he said.

"You will?" Both Whitney and Ruby sounded as surprised as he felt.

He hadn't meant to agree to go. But the look on Ruby's face, her disdain at the idea of a chilly winter stroll . . .

He refused to be that person.

He didn't care about the Christmas lights or decorations. He wasn't going to ooh and aah over the display. He was going because even Eeyore spent time with his friends.

Daniel shrugged. "Sure. I could use the exercise."

nine

WHITNEY LOOKED AWAY from Daniel quickly and pulled her scarf over her nose.

He raised his eyebrows. "What?"

Thankful her cheeks were probably already red from the evening breeze, she mumbled, "Nothing." It wouldn't do to get caught staring at him. Again.

It was just that she hadn't seen this version of him before. Not even at the market in that silly turkey hat.

He was wearing jeans, and she'd glimpsed the uni sweatshirt under his puffy coat before he zipped it up. The bright red toque pulled low over his ears covered the thought wrinkles his forehead usually sported.

And, if she wasn't mistaken, there was a hint of a smile at the corners of his mouth. No, that wasn't quite right. He wasn't smiling, but he was clearly relaxed. Which was quite a feat given the four-year-old tugging on his hand.

"Come on, Mr. Daniel. We can't be late." Julia Mae's voice chirped from somewhere deep in her parka as her snow pants swished with hurried steps.

"We don't have to rush," Whitney said, shooting Daniel an apologetic smile. "Your brother is with your mom. He's not going anywhere until we get there."

The little girl stopped, pressing her hands to her hips, staring pointedly at them both. "But the sooner we get there, the sooner we can see the lights."

"Of course," Daniel said. "Lead on."

Julia Mae required no further invitation, bounding along the boardwalk toward the center of town. Her roly-poly figure swung into and out of the pools of lamplight that glittered across the day-old snow, which had been pushed into piles against the embankment. Endless energy. Constant certainty.

"She always knows what she wants, doesn't she?" Daniel said.

"And where she's going." Whitney chuckled. "It must be nice."

He let out a low snort. "Jealous of a four-year-old?"

Yes. But she wasn't going to admit that. "Have you ever been that confident?"

"What makes you think I'm not?" His tone took on a hard edge, like he was a goalie tending his net.

Suddenly she couldn't blink. Her eyes ached in the cold as she stared at his profile. She must have forgotten how to walk too, because he was four steps ahead of her before she scurried to catch up. "Daniel, I'm so sorry. I didn't mean—"

He held up a gloved hand as she reached his side. When he looked down at her, the corners of his eyes crinkled. She almost missed the subtle movement behind his glasses because the rest of his face remained perfectly impassive. But right there—in the crow's feet she'd assumed he'd gotten from hours of study—was all the evidence she needed.

"You're teasing me," she announced with a playful push against the sleeve of his coat.

He shrugged, his shoulders twice as wide as normal. "Maybe." Still no smile. But the timbre of his voice had turned a distinct corner from Serious Street to Ludicrous Lane.

Infuriating man. How was a person supposed to know if he was making a joke if he never smiled? She'd have to spend every day studying him to figure him out. And she didn't have time for that.

She didn't want to do it either, of course.

Even if she did long for a chance to catch his blue eyes sparkling and his lips curving up. If she just kept watching him, maybe she could.

But she couldn't watch him when she was supposed to be watching her young charges. So she swung her gaze onto Julia Mae as the little girl pranced along the empty walkway. Her arms stuck out at an odd angle, and her legs were forced into a waddle.

"It seems like you know what you're doing and where you're going."

She jolted at his statement, and her eyes must have revealed her confusion.

"I mean with culinary school." Daniel tipped his head until the pom on his toque flopped forward. "And your business. It seems like you have a good plan to make your dreams come true."

"Right. Uh-huh."

"You don't?"

"I do. Just said so." Which did not explain why her steps suddenly quickened and she was in a rush to pick up Jack.

"Yes . . ." He dragged the word across the harbor and back. "It sounded like maybe you . . . Did I misunderstand?"

His words were so earnest, his gaze so intent that she couldn't ignore him—even if she wanted to. With a slow shake of her head, she sighed. "No."

Daniel opened his mouth, then closed it as his eyebrows met just north of his boxy glasses.

Not surprising. She wasn't exactly making sense to herself either. Which was going to make this explanation one for the record books. One for the rattling, unintelligible record books.

There was no way a guy like Daniel would understand what had prompted her to decide on culinary school. Or prompted her to decide anything at all. But his eyes glowed with interest nonetheless.

With a shallow breath, she tried to formulate a short story. Beginning. Middle. End. She'd learned at least that much during her Woodward and Bernstein phase. All three weeks of newspaper her junior year of high school.

She started at the beginning—or at least, *a* beginning.

"My dad said he was tired of bailing me out every time I changed direction."

"So . . . culinary school?"

"So, something." She twisted her mittens around her fingers. "Anything, really. Something I could stick with. Something I'm reasonably capable of."

He paused, digging the toe of his boot into a pile of snow that marked the end of the boardwalk. The white church steeple beckoned across the street, and Julia Mae gestured excitedly as her mom and brother exited through the double front doors. "Come on," she called.

With a shrug, Whitney darted after her, snagged her little gloved hand, and ran across the street.

Marie scooped her girl into her arms and asked in a hushed tone, "Are you excited to see the lights?"

"Uh-huh. And the mam-ger scene."

"Manger," Marie corrected her.

Julia Mae shrugged as though she'd heard it both ways. Then she pulled loose of her mom, grabbed her brother's hand, and waddled toward the sidewalk.

"Thank you for taking them to see Mr. Huntington's." Marie wrapped her arms around her middle, shivering in only her cream-colored sweater. "Brooke needed me to cover the extra rehearsal for the soloists, and surprisingly Jack didn't want to stick around."

Whitney chuckled. "Of course. Happy to. I haven't seen his new set."

Marie's gaze shifted toward the boardwalk, her eyes growing wide. A knowing smirk followed. "I see you're not going alone."

Whitney didn't even need to look over her shoulder to know that Daniel had caught up. When she did anyway, he was all the way to her side, and she stumbled a few steps back. An uneven snowdrift caught her off guard, and she began to tumble. Until Daniel caught her elbow, setting her back to rights as though he did it every day.

He caught her eye, and something warm zipped through her. Straight from her chest to the tips of her toes inside two layers of wool socks.

It was definitely a by-product of nearly falling over. Undoubtedly.

"We should, you know, get going." Whitney suddenly felt out of breath, so she pointed toward the kids and darted in their direction. She barely heard Marie's low chuckle and Daniel's much more formal farewell as she ushered the kids down the sidewalk. Their little faces were already glowing in the colorful Christmas bulbs that lined the eaves of the

Rathbones' one-story cottage. Eyes wide and little feet hopping with joy, they soaked in the merriment.

The Gingersols had lived next to the Rathbones for as long as Whitney could remember. They'd also insisted on outpacing their neighbors' Christmas decor for just as long.

Though she'd never heard a peep confirming such a thing, Whitney suspected that the Rathbones had dialed their decorations down to a single strand of oversized bulbs at the roofline so that the aging Mr. Gingersol didn't risk climbing onto his roof.

It didn't seem to matter to the kids. Every home received equal praise from the little critics. Wide eyes, gaping mouths, and cheers of excitement.

As they strolled the several blocks toward Mr. Huntington's home, Whitney let herself relax into the silent night, into the simple beauty of the village. It smelled of recent snow and wood fires, and she closed her eyes to enjoy the scent for a long second.

"Why are you working so hard to pay for culinary school if you don't want to go?"

She sucked in a sharp breath, the air achingly cold as it reached her lungs. She should have known Daniel would circle back to their conversation.

Shuffling her feet against the broken pavement of the narrow sidewalk, she frowned. "I have to do something with my life."

"Don't you want to want to do what you chose, though?"

She snorted. "That was all sorts of creative grammar."

He held up his hands in a retreat gesture. "I'm a numbers guy. Never said I was any good with words."

"Fair enough." Whitney shoved her trembling hands into the pockets of her coat.

"But don't you?"

She didn't think she'd get away with pretending she'd forgotten the question, so she tried another tactic. "Do you love being an accountant?"

"I'm not an accountant. I'm a CFO." Her eyebrow rose, and he quickly modified his statement. "I'm about to be a CFO."

"Okay, and is that what you always dreamed of doing?"

Those little lines above the bridge of his nose returned, his lips pinching together. "Maybe not. But I like numbers. I like how predictable they are. I like how they never lie."

"But they can be manipulated."

A muscle at the corner of his jaw jumped as deep lines appeared on either side of his lips. "We were talking about you and your dreams."

Whitney sidestepped a crack in the sidewalk, crunching into a snow-covered lawn. "And then we were talking about yours."

He shook his head hard. "Not anymore."

"Fine." She rolled her eyes toward the pale black sky above. Clouds had unfurled across the expanse, hiding the stars and reflecting the glow of the festive lights below.

It wasn't really fine, though—having to reveal her worst trait to someone who actually had his life together. She sucked in a steeling breath through the knitted fibers of her scarf and shared anyway. "There are too many options."

His head cocked, his question unspoken.

"What if I choose one thing and miss out on something I would have liked better?"

"Like a fear of missing out?"

Ducking her chin, she said, "Not exactly. It's more like, I'm not sure what I want, so I try a little of everything."

"*Little* being the operative word there?"

"Yeah. A month here. A few weeks there." Whitney stepped to the side to keep her eyes on her little charges half a block ahead. "I've been like this since I was their age. I played on a youth soccer team for all of thirty-seven minutes when I was seven."

"Thirty-seven? That's pretty specific."

She chuckled at the memory. "I took a ball directly to the face shortly before the end of a forty-five-minute practice and promptly decided that soccer was not for me."

She waited for him to smile at her poor athletic abilities, but he said only, "That makes sense."

"There were a string of clubs in junior high and high school. Theater. Choir. Mathletes."

His eyebrows rose, his eyes shining with clear interest at her mention of numbers.

"Not so fast. I stuck with that for exactly two meetings. Solving math problems under pressure was not my thing."

"So then, how does that lead to culinary school?"

She shook her head at the memory of her dad's stony face when he had sat her down four months before. "My parents wanted to retire—and they wanted to know that I could take care of myself." With a lift of one shoulder, she continued. "I've been baking something or another since I was in high school. I even made it all the way through a summer cooking class at the Red Door. So I figured . . . it seemed like the safest option."

"But not your dream?"

"I don't even know if I have a dream."

She expected him to look shocked, maybe to stop dead in his tracks. Who didn't have a dream for their life?

Whitney Garrett. Nice to meet you.

But Daniel didn't say anything. He didn't trip or even slow his pace. They strolled in silence for several long seconds, his gaze sweeping over the rows of lights on a green house. She wasn't even sure he'd heard her until he said, "Clearly Marie and Seth trust you to care for their kids. There must be a reason for that. What have you stuck with?"

His question wasn't accusatory or biting. But it stuck in her chest all the same, pinching a nerve deep inside, demanding an answer. Maybe it wasn't so much that *he* deserved an answer. *She* did. And she'd never been able to give herself one.

With a shake of her head, she sighed. "I don't know."

"I bet you can think of at least something." His voice carried a note that warmed her from the inside out, but she didn't have even a moment to enjoy it.

"Miss Whitney, hurry up! We're almost there!" The kids had stopped at the end of the sidewalk and waited impatiently, hopping from foot to foot, dancing with unrestrained excitement.

She couldn't blame them. Tugging on Daniel's sleeve, she began to run. "Come on."

They rounded a small bend in the road, and the whole street suddenly glowed.

Mr. Huntington had outdone himself. Again. Every year bigger and brighter. Every year more beautiful than the last.

Julia Mae squealed with delight, her clapping hands muffled by woolen mittens. Her joy, however, could not be stifled. "Jack. Jack. Jack. Look!"

She needn't have prompted him. His little brown eyes were wide, mouth open in silent wonder. Even Daniel's expression matched.

The two-story home sat back from its neighbors. Each

window was draped in flickering white lights that chased each other around the exterior. Faux icicles hung from the eaves, descending blue lights making them appear to drip to the row of bushes before the wraparound front porch. Colors exploded from the hedges, reds and blues and pinks and yellows netted across the rounded plants.

The usually white siding had turned molasses brown, the door bright white and sporting a wreath of green boughs adorned with a floppy red bow. Colorful dots covered the sloped roof, connecting every shingle. Waist-high candy canes marked a path around the side of the house, the stone steps clearly red and green gumdrops. The snow sprinkled across the lawn couldn't have been more perfectly piped.

"It's a ginber-bread house," Julia Mae announced, racing along the path. "I bet there's candy in the barn!"

Sure enough, Mr. Huntington had left a bucket of classic red and white candy canes along the path. Jack and Julia Mae barely slowed to pick theirs up, tear into the plastic, and suck on the end.

Just as the little girl made the turn around the side of the house, Jack snagged her hand, pulling her to a quick stop. When Whitney caught up with them, she saw why. The doors of the barn-shaped shed stood wide open, embracing a life-size nativity scene. Joseph with his staff stood protector over a kneeling Mary, who cradled baby Jesus beside the manger. Wise men, shepherds, donkeys, and sheep surrounded them.

Fifteen feet above them all, a bright star cast its glow. Strings of white bulbs reached from the top point of the star to the ground, encircling the scene.

An internal light shone from the heart of every single figure, illuminating the straw spread across the ground, glowing with hope. From the depths of the barn came a soft medley of "Silent Night" and other Christmas carols.

It could have been cheesy or commercialized. It wasn't. It was an invitation into a sacred moment.

"Whoa." The word seemed to escape from Daniel without his consent. It didn't come with a laugh or even a hint of a grin. But there was a subtle relaxation to the lines of his face, which had been so strained the last few days.

Whitney let herself just breathe in the scene. Fresh snow and pine. Laughter and life. It filled her to the brim, overflowing in gentle waves of peppermint-scented joy.

Maybe she didn't always know what she was supposed to do. But right now, right this minute, she was where she was supposed to be.

She could have stood there through the night, so long as there was darkness and light to break it. Daniel didn't seem any more eager to move on.

After several long minutes, Julia Mae sighed. "I'm cold."

Jack quickly agreed, and only then did Whitney realize the wind had bitten through her coat, making her teeth chatter and her muscles stiff.

The kids moved a lot slower going than they had coming, and Julia Mae soon lagged behind. Whitney was afraid she'd have to pick the girl up, but Daniel beat her to it, scooping the round figure into his arms. Julia Mae made no protest, and within a few steps, her head fell against his shoulder, her eyes drifting shut.

For the briefest moment, Whitney thought she saw the hint of a smile break through his stone facade.

Yep. This was exactly where she was supposed to be.

ten

DANIEL COULDN'T FIND anything wildly amiss with his aunt's recordkeeping. He also couldn't shake the feeling that she was trying to dig into his personal life.

The latter made confirming the former a little bit harder because every time he opened his laptop to finish reviewing the last ledgers, Aretha showed up with a plate of sugar cookies, a knowing wink, and prying questions. That morning, he hadn't been successful in dodging them.

"What do you think of Ruby?" Aretha asked after the three of them finished their pancake breakfast. Ruby had excused herself to make some phone calls, leaving Daniel to face his aunt's interrogation.

He shrugged. "I think she works for a company with questionable ethics. I'm not sure that's a high recommendation."

Aretha frowned for a moment, then waved off his concern. "You said she's working to resolve that issue."

Yes, for the sake of keeping the store's reputation intact and making the acquisition. Not necessarily because it was the decent thing to do. Everything R & R did was in their best interest—to benefit their bottom line.

He didn't blame them. Exactly. Businesses had to make a profit. And conglomerates didn't grow by being laissez-faire with their plans.

"I like her. She's smart." Aretha waited a beat. When he didn't respond, she poked one of his arms, which were crossed on the table before him. "Don't you think?"

"I suppose so." They'd compared résumés early on, and hers was definitely impressive. Top of her business school class, top-tier internships, and a rapid rise up the corporate ladder.

"And pretty too."

He rolled his eyes.

"I wish I had hair like that. So smooth and silky."

He was tempted to roll his eyes again and quickly said, "I prefer curly hair."

Aretha's thin cheeks turned pink, and she patted her short hair with both hands. "Yeah?"

Her gray curls hadn't been the ones to jump to mind, but he couldn't contradict the compliment. "Jack was no fool to snatch you up."

"Oh, you do tell tales." She may have denied it, but she giggled like a schoolgirl anyway. "Speaking of, I'm supposed to meet him at the store. Will you and"—her gaze darted toward the stairs—"Ruby be by later? Maybe after lunch." An arched eyebrow suggested that he could take Ruby out for said meal.

His aunt wasn't nearly as subtle as she thought she was. If he could pick up on her insinuation, then anyone could. Unless he had misunderstood, which wasn't outside the realm of possibility. Maybe Aretha just wanted to make sure the deal went through.

With a noncommittal shrug, he said, "We'll stop by. I have some emails to review for work first."

"Oh, that. You haven't officially started yet," Aretha said as she strolled toward the front door. "You should enjoy your vacation."

Vacation. Right. Was that what this was? Funny. He was working awfully hard for a vacation.

An image of Whitney's face glowing in the Christmas lights the night before flashed through his mind's eye, and his face pinched in a way it hadn't for a while. A tightness filled his cheeks as he stretched long-dormant muscles.

Her joy had been contagious, and she shone brighter even than Mr. Huntington's lights. When she saw the nativity scene, she'd gasped a little breath. He wasn't sure she even knew she'd done it. But it snapped something in his chest that had been mostly shut down for years, setting it alight.

He hadn't felt anything good about Christmas in years. There had been seething anger at first, but that had been mostly directed at Lauren. It had slowly faded to distaste. Then apathy had set in. Pretty much denial of the holiday in general. There were enough people groups in Toronto that didn't celebrate Christmas that he had always been able to find an open restaurant for takeout the day of.

He wasn't denying the birth of Jesus or what that meant. He just wasn't going to celebrate it on some arbitrary day in December that had literally nothing to do with the actual birth of the Savior.

Except last night had been different. He'd felt *something*. It wasn't sweet like fudge, but it was warm. Like hot cocoa in the evening chill, sliding down his throat and warming him from the inside out. That feeling certainly wasn't anything as overt as joy. But seeing the awe in the faces of those kids—Whitney's too—made his breath hitch.

Whatever he'd felt had been something like *wonder*.

The moment he identified it, it swelled around his heart again, easing through him, soft and smooth.

Daniel wasn't naive enough to think it would stick around, but for now he didn't mind experiencing why the card companies called this the most wonderful time of the year. And if he was fully honest, that meant he was enjoying his time on the island more than a little bit.

When he was officially on the clock for All Terrain, he would work most evenings. A few Saturdays. Probably Sundays too. That was what the executives at the small chain did. He had known that before accepting the position. It was worth it to enter the C-suite.

But maybe Aretha was right. He should enjoy his time while he could.

He would work for just a couple hours that morning. He could make the most of it by working in the corner of the dining room and avoiding further interruption. Out of the direct line of sight from the front door in case Aretha returned. Just close enough to the kitchen to hear Whitney's steady singing—all familiar Christmas carols. She didn't have a powerhouse voice or anything. It was soft and low, and filled with that same warmth he'd seen on her face the night before.

He had a feeling if she knew he could hear her, she'd put an immediate stop to her impromptu concert. So he set to work as quietly as he could.

Laptop open, he tried to answer a few general questions. All Terrain's communications director wanted a quote for the press release announcing his hire.

I'm pleased to join the team.

That sounded like he couldn't come up with anything more original.

He'd come back to that request.

The CEO wanted him to join a call with the shareholders this week. Sure.

He needed to review the next fiscal budget and suggest some cuts to make the stores more profitable.

Ah. He settled into his chair, sliding down into a posture that would get him in trouble with his mom. Earning an MBA and turning twenty-nine did not pardon him from his mother's scolding. But she wasn't here. And a quick check around the room revealed that Aretha hadn't come back either.

An hour later, he'd come up with at least three changes that would almost certainly increase profitability. He was busy typing up his notes when the carol he'd been humming along to from the kitchen suddenly stopped.

"Aaaaahhh! No!"

He snapped his head toward the kitchen door, his neck stiff as he waited for a crash. The silence was worse. He slammed his laptop closed and launched himself toward the kitchen door, setting off the bell as he swung through it to find Whitney still as stone. In fact, she looked a lot like a statue, her hand held before her and her eyes locked on oddly glistening fingertips. Corkscrew curls at her temples had escaped the haphazard ponytail at the nape of her neck, and her wide eyes eclipsed the rest of her face.

"Whitney?" She didn't respond, so he leaned forward, taking cautious steps across the kitchen. "Are you all right?"

He made it three more steps in her direction before she seemed to realize she wasn't alone. She blinked and whipped her hand behind her back. "Daniel. I'm sorry if I bothered you."

He glanced toward the dining room where he'd left his work and shook his head quickly. "Not at all. What's going on? Did you cut yourself?"

"No." She shook her head once. Firmly.

He pursed his lips to the side, and she could probably tell that he didn't believe her.

Slowly she brought her hand from behind her back. No evidence of blood, but the fist she made was awkward at best. Her fingers were coated in something shiny that looked plenty sticky. She pinched her first two fingers to her thumb over and over.

"What is that?" he asked when it was clear she wasn't going to say more.

Ducking her chin, she mumbled under her breath.

"What?" He leaned in again.

"Butter. Okay? It's butter."

He scanned the counters for any indication of how it had ended up all over her hand, but they were perfectly clean, save two rows of pies cooling on racks and space for more that were presumably in the oven.

Suddenly the timer on the oven chirped.

Her eyes grew large, but he was already sliding his hands into the oven mitts sitting on the island. "You wash your hands. I'll get the pies."

When he opened the bottom oven door, his glasses immediately fogged over, leaving him enveloped in the scent of heaven. He couldn't imagine anything smelling better than the desserts. Brown sugar, cinnamon, and a slew of spices as familiar as home.

When his glasses finally cleared enough for him to see, he

pulled four pies from the bottom oven and four more from the top. Each as golden as Whitney's hair and enough to make a man's mouth water.

But Whitney looked decidedly less pleased with her efforts. She frowned at each pie in turn, slamming her hands against her hips in frustration. When she pressed against her right side, the pocket of her sweatshirt let out a distinct hiss.

Rolling her eyes, Whitney grumbled something under her breath that sounded like, "Stupid pie."

He'd never seen her in a foul mood. Honestly, that was his schtick, and he wasn't ready to pass the baton.

"You want to tell me what happened?"

"No." She puffed a few curls out of her face and sighed. "Not really. But fine." She gestured to the pies, then to the right pocket of her red sweatshirt. The color made her cheeks and nose look even more pink, and he had to fight a tick at the corner of his mouth. She sure was cute.

Blotting her forehead with the back of her hand, she melted into the edge of the island. "I forgot to set out my butter this morning. It needs time to soften before I use it. But it was kind of chilly in here, so I . . ." Her face broke, and she let out an adorable snort. "I put it in my pocket to warm it quicker. And I forgot all about it."

"Until you put your hand in your pocket."

"Yes." Her scowl didn't carry much weight as it fell apart under her laugh. "That was hours ago, and it's a melted mess in my pocket now."

His lips twitched. He couldn't help it. They stretched into a full smile that made his shoulders jerk with humor. Whitney's eyes flashed with a joy that matched the bubbling in his chest.

"What are you going to do with your pocket butter?"

"Pocket butter?"

"You got a better name for it?"

She laughed. "How about no name. The butter in my pocket gets no name. Zero recognition. It will never be mentioned again."

"Ah, that doesn't seem fair."

"To whom?" She dipped her chin and glared playfully up at him.

"To me."

Shaking her head, she turned back to the row of pies, steam still rising from their tops. "What am I going to do with these pies?"

"So pocket butter was supposed to go in the pies?"

She shot a hard look in his direction. "The butter that may or may not have met its demise in my pocket was indeed supposed to be used for the crusts. But when I forgot I had gotten it out, I started over on the recipes. And I may have added ingredients to a bowl that was already partially full. Jack asked me to go over his lines for the pageant with him this morning, so I did. And . . . I think I lost track. I honestly don't even know if they have bottom crusts."

Daniel shrugged. "Sell them as a low-carb option."

"What if they taste like *feet*?"

A laugh burst out of him.

Whitney whipped in his direction, eyes wide and unblinking. "I didn't think you knew how to laugh."

That didn't deserve a response. Of course he knew how. He just chose not to most of the time. He couldn't help it if Whitney's laugh was contagious. She was the one being ridiculous.

"So, what are you going to do with the pies?"

Covering her face with her hands, she looked up between slender fingers. "I don't suppose you might be willing . . ."

"Say less." He held out his hand, and she immediately

pulled a fork from the nearby drawer. He wasted no time cutting a small square from the edge of the pie nearest the sink.

"Blow on it. It's hot."

He lifted one eyebrow at her, and her cheeks turned even more pink.

"Sorry. Too much time with the kids."

He nodded his concession to her apology and did indeed blow on it. His breath made the spirals of steam dance over the row of treats, releasing even more of that heavenly scent. Inhaling once more, he took a careful bite, schooling his features to remain placid even as his tongue savored an explosion of flavor.

It was sweet and textured. Layers of spice only enhanced the naturally sweet apple slices. He wasn't a culinary critic—not by a long shot—but this was divine. Better than it smelled, even.

He couldn't hold back a groan.

"That bad?" she whispered, twisting a dish towel to within a breath of its life.

After swallowing, he paused. Then slowly he said, "Well, it doesn't taste like feet."

She snapped her towel playfully in his direction. "Daniel!"

He chuckled. "It doesn't need pocket butter. Or anything else, for that matter. It's perfect."

Whitney snatched the fork out of his hand, and he didn't know if he was more surprised that she'd taken it or offended that she'd stolen his opportunity for more of the pie. He hadn't shared silverware since . . . ever. But she didn't give him a chance to change her mind. She dug in and failed to cool her bite before shoving it into her mouth.

"Ah!" She let out a burst of steam, huffing and puffing to cool her tongue.

"Should have blown on it first."

She swatted him with the towel again while waving her other hand over her tongue. "Burned my taste buds," she squeaked.

"More for me, I guess." He stole the fork back and scooped up another bite, exaggerating the motion as he blew to cool it. "So good," he said around the bite.

"Jerk," she mumbled, but her smile didn't fade. "I'm not sure I should trust you, though."

"Maybe I should have lied so there's more for me."

Her eyebrows formed an uncertain *V*. "Just to be safe, I better ask Aretha when she gets back."

He shook his head as he shoveled in more pie. "She's at the store with Jack all afternoon. I'm supposed to meet up with her—me and Ruby are—later today."

The joy that had been so infectious only moments before slowly leaked out of Whitney. The spark in her eyes disappeared, her smile dimming a fraction. She tried to paste it back in place, but he wasn't fooled.

He'd said or done something wrong—though he wasn't sure what. The trouble was, he wasn't sure what to do with that knowledge. "Um . . ."

"You should definitely find Ruby. Maybe bring her a slice of pie so I can get a candid opinion."

Before he could figure out what to say or how to fix his mistake—whatever it had been—Whitney slid over one of the pies that had been on the counter when he entered, sliced it, and served a piece of it.

"Ruby gets a different pie?"

Whitney nodded. "Ruby gets a piece of cooled pie that won't fall apart on the plate and look like a complete mess." She held the white plate out to him with one hand and steered him toward the door with the other. "Go on. Take it to her."

eleven

"IS YOUR AUNT HERE?"

Whitney looked up from where she and the kids were cutting out snowflakes at the front table in the dining room. At the next table, Daniel glanced up too, his forehead still wrinkled in thought. It slowly eased as he focused his gaze on Ruby, who swung into the room.

Ruby's smile was wider than the Northumberland Strait and brighter than a galaxy of stars. With an expectant flip of her hand, she said, "Well?"

Daniel looked around the room. "No. I don't think so."

"Where is she?" Ruby shifted from foot to foot, her anticipation visible. "You have to get her here."

Pushing himself up, Daniel leaned forward, his hands flat against the table. "What happened?"

Ruby pressed a finger to her red lips. "Where's Aretha?"

He sighed but picked up his phone and quickly called his aunt. "Can you come over? . . . Yeah, Ruby has some news . . . All right. See you in a few." When he hung up, he looked up expectantly, as though by making the phone call he'd done enough to earn at least some of the news.

Ruby didn't agree. She shook her head and waltzed toward the kids. "What are you working on?"

"Snowflakes," Jack said, using his safety scissors to cut haphazard shapes from the artfully folded pieces of colorful paper.

"Can I make some too?"

Whitney nearly dropped her scissors but scrambled to find another pair beneath the loose papers strewn across the tabletop. When she handed them over, Ruby gracefully lowered herself into the chair beside Jack. Her lips were pursed in a secretive half smile.

"You're really not going to tell us?" Whitney whispered.

Ruby's smile faltered.

Whitney immediately recognized her misstep. She wasn't supposed to know about the situation—hypothetically or otherwise. And she had no stake in the store's acquisition.

"I—um—it just seems like you have good news. Don't you want to share it?"

Ruby relaxed as she folded a piece of paper in half and then in half again. "I'll wait."

Daniel had sat down again in front of his computer, but he couldn't seem to focus on whatever was on the screen. He picked up his finger as though he was going to type. Then paused. Suddenly his chair scraped across the floor as he swung it toward the end of the craft table. With a spin on one chair leg, he sat down backward, resting his arms across the back of the seat.

"Seriously?" His voice was low but prodding. "You're going to make us wait?"

Ruby batted her perfectly curved lashes and offered a flirty titter but didn't raise her head from the smooth motion of her scissors.

After several seconds of silence, Daniel grumbled, "Better give me some of those too."

Julia Mae immediately handed over her scissors, which were the perfect size for a four-year-old. In Daniel's hands, they looked like they belonged in a dollhouse.

Whitney shot him a sideways smile, and the corners of his eyes crinkled as he gave a couple practice snips with the blades that were about as likely as not to cut through the paper.

"Here, you can use this paper." Julia Mae passed him a crumpled red piece. "I folded it myself," she added, sitting up straighter on her knees.

"Thank you," he said and set to work sawing through the construction paper.

They were still enamored with paper snowflakes when Aretha arrived fifteen minutes later. The front door rattled when she slammed it closed, but she had to call to get their attention. "What's the news?"

Ruby jumped up from a pile of colorful confetti at her seat, Daniel right behind her.

"They agreed to new terms!" Ruby rushed forward and grabbed Aretha's hands.

"Without the quilts?" Aretha asked.

"No, they want the quilts, but they're committed to making the deal advantageous for all parties—including the quilters. I need to meet with the consignors to negotiate, but they'll build that into the price."

Aretha let out a swift breath before a smile broke across her face, and she scooped Ruby into a fierce hug. "Thank the good Lord." With a quick release, Aretha steered Ruby toward Daniel, who also received a warm hug.

Whitney tried to smile but found her face stiff in spite of the joyous news. This was what they wanted. This was the news Aretha had needed.

But the churning in her middle hadn't gotten that message, which insisted on turning over and over,.agitating the acid in her stomach until it bubbled like a sourdough starter.

"Is this good news, Meemee Retha?" Julia Mae asked, running toward her surrogate grandma and hugging her about the knees.

Aretha bent over and squeezed the girl. "Yes. This is very good news!"

There it was. Right from the source. This was *very good* news.

Whitney put that on repeat in her mind, praying her stomach would get the message—her face too. She didn't need a mirror to know that her features didn't reflect any of the same joy as Aretha's. Everything inside her had been pulled tight, a string tugging straight to the center of her chest and stealing her breath with it.

Logically, she knew that it had nothing to do with the news and everything to do with the way Ruby had slipped into Daniel's embrace. She fit there perfectly, his arms wrapped around her waist, holding her securely. Beneath his standard blue button-up, the muscles in his shoulders bunched when he squeezed her, releasing an even broader smile on Ruby's face.

Whitney couldn't see his face from this angle, but Ruby's stole what little breath she had left.

Which was absolutely ridiculous.

This was exactly what Aretha had said would happen. Exactly what Whitney was supposed to want too.

But she couldn't watch it anymore, so she ducked her

head and focused on the paper carnage across the table, brushing the litter into her open hand. Clearly a glutton for punishment, Whitney peeked up just as they stepped apart.

Ruby pressed to her tiptoes and planted a soft kiss on Daniel's cheek. "Thank you. We would have made a major misstep without you. Everyone at the office agreed."

Daniel gingerly touched the pads of his fingers to the spot where Ruby had pressed her lips as he looked over his shoulder.

Whitney jerked her chin away before he could catch her eye—inherently knowing he would seek her gaze out—and scooted her seat back as she searched for a reason to escape. "Come on, Jack. Help me clean this up."

"A little while longer," he pleaded, holding up a half-finished snowflake.

"All right. Okay. That's fine. I'll be right back."

Whitney flew to the kitchen and yanked the swinging door closed behind her. It flapped a couple times before the springs stopped, shutting out the happy buzz from the other room.

Throwing herself against the counter, she pressed her hands to her overheated cheeks, her eyes burning in an altogether unwelcome way. She was being stupid. Absolutely ridiculous.

She just couldn't turn off her reaction.

And she certainly wasn't going to analyze it to figure out why.

She sucked in a few deep breaths through her nose and rubbed her fists against her eyes.

"This is working out even better than I could have hoped!" Aretha announced in a stage whisper as the jingle bell on the door announced her entry. "Now they're going to—" She froze, her hands mid-dance above her head. "Honey? Are you all right?"

Whitney blinked, trying to focus her fuzzy vision, and managed a jerky nod. "Of course."

Aretha pressed a hand to her arm. "You look a little peaked. Are you sure?"

"Just a—uh—just a headache." She managed a wan smile. "But that's great news about the store."

Her eyebrows dancing up and down, Aretha giggled. "Even better news about Daniel and Ruby."

"Oh?" Whitney pressed a hand to her middle as the churning dough starter returned.

"Well, now they'll have to meet with all of my consignors, and some of them aren't local. That means more time together. More opportunity for sparks to fly."

More opportunity for Ruby to kiss him again.

More opportunity for Daniel to realize how much he liked it. How much he liked her.

The headache she'd fudged a moment before suddenly pounded very real behind her eyes. "Right. Good."

"I knew she'd come through. She really worked to make things right, even though it was my mistake." She steepled her fingers beneath her chin. "I knew I liked her from the beginning. She'll be so good for him. Did you see? He almost smiled."

"You're very perceptive," Whitney agreed. She hadn't seen Daniel smile today, but she had heard his actual laugh after the pocket butter incident.

And that had been because of her. Okay, it had been because of her silly mistake. But still, he'd joined *her* in laughter. The only hint of it in the weeks he'd been on the island.

But he certainly hadn't pushed Ruby away today. He'd held her long and close. And that kiss . . .

"Honey, you don't look good. Why don't you go home and lie down?"

She began to argue that someone needed to stay with the kids, but Aretha cut her off. "I'll watch Julia Mae and Jack until Seth gets home. You go take care of yourself."

She gave a mute nod. She could go home, but she had no idea how she was supposed to take care of whatever irrationality had settled on her. Because Daniel had found a place in her mind, and he didn't seem eager to vacate it.

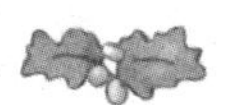

Daniel looked up from his spot on the couch in the parlor with every creak of the floor. He hadn't seen Whitney in three days, and he was beginning to think it might be intentional on her part. He'd seen evidence of her in the inn's kitchen. He'd even tasted evidence of her work—savoring a particularly tasty breakfast hash that very morning. But Marie had delivered it. As Seth had the day before.

They'd made some excuses about Whitney needing to get to another farmers' market. But there couldn't be one every day this week.

If he was honest with himself, he'd hoped she would ask him to help her again. They'd made a good team in Summerside.

And where else could he wear his turkey toque?

But the creak from the floorboard in the hallway wasn't Whitney. Ruby appeared beneath the mistletoe instead, her eyes bright. "There you are. I thought maybe you'd gone to the shop."

He shook his head. Which was the extent of the response that she allowed.

"So, I was thinking about the quilters that we need to meet with. I have a drafted agreement for them." She waved a single sheet of paper as she dropped to the couch right beside him. "What do you think of this section? I was thinking that it leaves the door open for future sales to the store but at negotiable rates."

Daniel tried to scoot closer to the armrest to give her more room as she rattled on. She only leaned in closer, holding the page in front of him and reading the section in question.

"I was thinking that we should give ourselves at least ninety minutes for each appointment. I doubt it'll take that long, but we're working with artists, not businesswomen. We might need to explain some of the details."

He nodded slowly. But instead of agreement, a suggestion popped out of his mouth, evidence of what had been on his mind. "I think we should bring Whitney with us."

The paper wilted as she swung toward him. "What? Why?"

"It was her idea."

Ruby leaned back and squinted up at him. "What was?"

"She's the one who told me that the community would push back if they felt like R & R was taking advantage of the quilters or the store."

Cocking her head, Ruby frowned. "But we don't need her. She'll be bored. And it could just make the appointments take longer. Anyway, doesn't she have work to do here, watching the kids?"

Daniel sighed. All of those things were true. But he had to come up with some way to spend time with Whitney.

Ruby opened her mouth to say something else, but a little voice replaced her smooth soprano.

"Mr. Daniel! We're going sledding. You have to come with us!"

They both swung toward the round figure waddling into the room. Julia Mae took in his open laptop and the paperwork on the coffee table trunk and then visibly ignored all evidence that he was working. She also ignored Ruby.

"Juli-a!" Footfalls raced down the hall. First small ones, then grown-up ones. Then the whole gang was there. First Little Jack, then a panting Whitney. They were all decked out in their snow gear, mittens hanging from strings on the ends of their sleeves—even Whitney.

The kids' faces were bright, and their grown-up was prettier than usual. Her pink cheeks and sweet smile were like pie to a man on a forced diet. And he devoured the sight of her.

She caught his gaze, her smile growing. Then her eyes darted back and forth between him and Ruby, the corners of her mouth beginning to droop.

Daniel jumped up, attempting a smile. If he managed it, Whitney didn't see it, her head already bent over her charges. "Come on, guys. We've been over this. We can't bother them when they're working."

"But Mr. Daniel wants to go with us." Julia Mae lifted pleading eyes toward him. "Don't you?"

I'm sorry, Whitney mouthed, her perfect pink lips forming the words so precisely that he thought he'd actually heard them.

"You're going sledding?"

Jack nodded vigorously. "Miss Whitney says that we can go on the big hill because Jessie's with Mom today. It's going to be so fun."

Daniel had no doubt it would be. And he suddenly wanted in on it. Or at least in on the chance to spend some more time with Whitney. She couldn't avoid him if he was hanging out with her charges.

He frowned down at his button-up and khaki pants. They would never withstand an afternoon in the snow. He'd borrowed a pair of jeans from Big Jack when they'd gone to see the lights. "You think Papa Jack has a pair of snow pants he'd loan me?"

The kids cheered, but Whitney stared at him with a blank face.

Maybe a couple hours together in the snow would help him figure out why she'd been dodging him.

twelve

"YOU NEXT. YOU NEXT!"

Whitney looked down at the little girl tugging on her hand, a frown already in place. "Oh, no. I don't think that would be wise."

"Come on, Miss Whitney." Jack spun the toboggan around, pointing it down the smooth slope between towering pines. "You have to go at least once. You said you would."

She crossed her arms as far as her puffy jacket would allow and stared down her nose at him. "I do not recall saying any such thing."

The shadow that fell beside her shifted, and Daniel let out a soft snort. "I think you did." His voice was deep but outlined with a chuckle.

She spun toward him, her snow pants hissing, and pressed her fists against the padding over her hips. "First of all, I would remember something like that. And second of all"—she tried to hold up two fingers, but her mittens prevented anyone from seeing her emphasis—"you said you'd sled. Not me."

Daniel rubbed his face, and she couldn't tell if he was trying to wipe away a smile or keep his features warm. She kind of missed the black glasses he usually wore at the inn. Without them the challenge in his eyes was clear. But so was the laughter, which made her smile. His head tilted toward the sled as he lifted his pale brown eyebrows.

She opened her mouth to make another point—that she would never, ever agree to go sledding again—but was quickly interrupted.

"You said *we* could go sledding." Julia Mae frowned. "Aren't you part of *we*?"

She wanted to bite off her own tongue for being so loose that morning. "No, I meant I would take you sledding. I would walk with you and watch you and freeze my nose off while *you* sailed down the hill."

There was no way she was getting on that little death trap. Nope. She'd done that one too many times.

And she'd seen her life flash before her eyes as she plowed into a pine tree.

Her elbow ached at just the memory, the echo of the snapping bones in her arm deep in her ears, quickly followed by her mother's reprimand as they waited in the emergency room. "What on earth were you thinking? You're seventeen years old. Of all the things you've tried, you pick the most dangerous. It's a miracle you didn't break your neck. What made you think you should go sledding?"

Whitney had mumbled something under her breath. And not the truth.

The truth was infinitely more embarrassing than the broken bones. She'd gone only because Randy Billings had invited her. So handsome. Tall as a church steeple and leaner than a lupin. And those brown eyes, richer than dark chocolate.

Sledding with him had been fun. What she remembered of it before slamming into the tree trunk, anyway.

The doctor had told her if she ever broke her arm in the same spot again, she would need a surgery that could damage the nerves in her right arm and make her lose the use of her fingers.

That was the end of her sledding career.

And no amount of pouting from her little charges was going to change that.

Or challenges from handsome men.

Her stomach dropped as she stared at Daniel. He *was* handsome. Even more than Randy had been to her teenage eyes.

She had zero business noticing that. Again.

She needed to wipe that realization fully from her brain. If only his crinkling crow's feet, perfectly proportioned features, and full lower lip didn't insist on reminding her every time she glanced in his general direction.

"No." She shook her head and clapped her mittens together. "You kids go again. It's cold out here, so you've got to keep moving."

"Ah, Miss Whitney," Jack whined. "Come on. It's fun."

"I'm sure it is. So get on with it." She tugged Jack's cap a little lower over his ears and then scooped up Julia Mae and deposited her on the toboggan.

"Fine." Jack jumped on behind her. "We'll show you how." The last of his words disappeared on the wind as the two swooped down the hill. Laughter split the air as they reached the flat ground and bailed out into the soft snow.

"It does look kind of fun."

The whisper in her ear made her jump, and Whitney had to force herself not to step away from him. She couldn't have him thinking he unnerved her. Or that she'd desperately needed space after seeing him and Ruby together.

"Fun for the kids," she said.

"You don't like to have fun?"

"Ha!" She spun toward him then, taking him in from the tip of his toque to the borrowed snow boots on his feet. "You're one to be talking."

He shrugged. At least, that was what she assumed he did under the thick lining of Seth's parka.

"You sure haven't been having much fun at the inn."

His eyes went wide. "That's quite an assumption." His words came out on a puff of cold air.

She snorted. "Oh, come on. You've either been working or . . . or hanging out with the kids."

He nodded slowly, his voice dropping. "Or with you."

Her stomach dropped. Goose bumps that had absolutely nothing to do with the weather and everything to do with the timbre of his voice covered her arms.

They had spent a fair bit of time together. But he was supposed to be spending it with Ruby.

He puffed another clouded breath. "Not so much lately."

"What's that supposed to mean?"

"Have you been avoiding me? I haven't seen you in days."

"That's not true. I've been . . ." Her tongue knotted up on the lie she desperately wanted to tell, and she steered away from it. "This isn't about me. You're the one who's barely smiled since you got to the island."

As if to prove her point, he frowned. "That's not true."

"It is." The memory of his crinkled crow's feet and resonant chuckle washed over her. "Well, except for that mishap."

"You mean the Great Pocket Butter Incident of—"

She scowled, and he rewarded her with a dazzling grin,

flashing those perfect teeth and for the first time revealing a shallow dimple in his left cheek that was nearly hidden by the couple days of beard growth.

"I don't think it deserves anywhere near that level of acclaim."

"Sure. Keep telling yourself that."

She was searching for a suitable retort when two little voices joined them, chattering over each other.

"That was so fun!"

"You have to try it!"

"No," Whitney replied without hesitation.

Julia Mae's bottom lip poked out. Then her eyes got bright, and she tugged on Whitney's pant leg. "I wasn't scared at all because Jack was with me. Mr. Daniel can go with you!"

Whitney felt her face pale, even below her weather-chapped nose and cheeks. "I don't think he wants to go either."

But Daniel's lips curled into a wicked grin. "I'll go if you will."

"Yes!" Jack pumped his fist and hopped around in a circle.

"I . . . I can't," she started, but Julia Mae was already tugging her the three steps to the sled.

"Mr. Daniel won't let you get hurt."

Sure. Keep thinking that, kid. Daniel was no guarantee of safety. Besides, being close enough to share a sled invited all sorts of other issues—like a swarm of butterflies in her chest she'd rather not have to deal with.

But somehow she was already sinking onto the toboggan, her stomach twisting in a painful knot. She hugged her arms across her body and sat as far back as she could, saying a little prayer that the snow would melt. Immediately.

She blinked.

Nope. It was still there, twinkling in the sun. And she was still headed toward what would surely be her demise.

Daniel tapped her shoulder. "You'll have to move forward if you want me to go with you."

Heat flushed at her neck. "Oh. Right." But she didn't move. Maybe if she stayed put, he couldn't go with her. Then there was no deal.

With a gentle shove, he scooted her forward, and her plan was foiled. Her knees met her chin as Jack handed her the lead rope, and she shot him a wicked glare. "I'm going to get you back for this, little man."

Jack cackled with glee, his feet stomping a little dance of delight. Julia Mae's eyes practically glowed with excitement. Probably at the possibility of seeing her nanny end up in an epic crash.

Suddenly her wooden seat shifted, and a squeak escaped her. Clapping a mitten over her mouth, Whitney concentrated on the hill and held as still as possible as a big body settled behind her. His thighs squeezed her hips as he wedged his boots against the curled front of the sled.

"You okay there, Miss Whitney?" Daniel spoke directly into her ear, his warm breath finding its way to her neck through her hair beneath the edge of her toque and sending a solitary shiver all the way down her spine.

Another flush of heat—this one entirely different from the last—washed over her, replacing the freezing wind for just a moment. Even her tingling nose felt the rush of warmth before it vanished as quickly as her breath in the air.

She managed a stilted nod despite the riot in every single one of her muscles.

"Lean back a little," he said.

Right. Yes. Getting closer would help this situation. If there was any helping it.

She should get up and march back to the inn, wrangling her charges with her. They couldn't force her.

Instead, she let out a slow breath, managing to relax into him. Well, that was a bit of a stretch. Through layers of puffy coats and slippery snow pants, she couldn't feel much of him. Just his breath on her neck. Steady. Even. Reassuring.

"Are you . . ." He paused, brushing her braid over to the side. "You're shaking. Are you scared?" He kept his voice low enough that the kids, who had thrown themselves into a nearby drift to make snow angels, couldn't hear. "I thought you were just playing with the kids."

She had been playing with them. And maybe she hadn't wanted them to know that the memory of her last sledding incident made her stomach flip. In a decidedly unpleasant way.

She didn't need the kids to know.

"I'm freezing."

He snorted at that, a hint of humor filling the sound. But he wrapped one of his arms around her middle and took the rope from her with the other as though she was all in. "I'll steer."

Probably wise. Not that she was going to admit that to him. Her aim had certainly been off the last time she'd flown down this hill.

"Ready?"

She shook her head, the hill stretching out before her, the trees lining the run creeping ever closer until the path was narrower than the sled. Until they were guaranteed to crash. Until she was guaranteed another broken arm, the inability to bake another pie that month, and an end to her culinary school plans.

The air froze in her lungs, and it had nothing to do with the temperature. Scrambling to find her footing, she fought his arm, but it didn't budge.

"No. This is a bad idea. I don't—"

"Too late." Daniel chuckled. Giving her a quick squeeze, he rocked against her back, and the toboggan took off.

Her stomach left her body as they tipped over the edge and flew down the slope. Jack and Julia Mae shouted, but she could barely hear them over the shriek that ripped from her own throat as she pressed her mittens over her eyes. The wind whipped across her cheeks. Freezing. Stinging. Life-giving.

Without warning her scream turned to laughter as they swished over the packed snow, the trees stepping back a safe distance.

Daniel was an expert navigator, steering them over the uneven terrain with ease. With each bump, he squeezed her a little tighter, held her a bit more secure. She was enveloped by him. Front, back, and sides.

She dropped her hands in time to see the bottom of the hill hurtling toward them, but she'd never felt quite so protected.

Until he pressed his lips to her ear.

"You ready?"

"For—" But there wasn't time to ask what he was planning before he yanked the rope to the right just as they hit a bump. Daniel tugged her to the left, and the toboggan vanished as they went airborne.

Squeezing her eyes closed, she waited for the searing pain in her elbow. Or anywhere else in her body. But it didn't come. Instead, a puff of the white stuff cradled her as she landed in a snowdrift.

Her heart slammed against her ribs. Once. Twice. A third time for good measure. She tried to suck in a breath, but

Daniel had managed to land mostly sprawled on top of her, and there was no room for her lungs to expand.

"You all right there, Miss Whitney?" His voice held something strange. Something she hadn't heard in it before. Something warm.

"Can't. Breathe," she wheezed, trying to push him off.

His eyes crinkled at the corners, though his mouth didn't move. Pressing a glove next to her face, he pushed himself up, only for the snow to give way under his hand. He landed on top of her again, face-to-face, both of them letting out matching groans.

Whitney burst out laughing with the only air left in her lungs. If this was how she was going to die, she was glad to go out on a giggle.

"Sorry 'bout that," he said as he managed to roll off her. At least far enough for her to grab a breath.

"Seemed pretty intentional to me."

His gaze flicked in the direction of the vanished sled, then slipped guiltily back to meet hers, his teeth flashing in the sun. "Well, not all of it."

"Suuure."

Suddenly his smile vanished, the glow in his eyes dimming to something more thoughtful. He bit the finger of his glove and pulled his hand free before brushing at a particularly cold patch on her cheek. His thumb left a trail of steam, and whatever snow had been there was gone with his touch.

Still her cheeks burned, which had nothing to do with the cold and everything to do with the man hovering so close. The one still pressing his warm hand to her face.

The corner of his mouth ticked up in a half smile, and it was a switch to release the butterflies inside. They dived and glided, more powerful even than when he'd sent the two of them over the hill.

"I didn't hurt you, did I?" His gaze swooped down her jacket, confirming that she was whole.

Definitely whole in body. Maybe not so much in mind, all things considered.

She shook her head and shimmied in the snow as evidence.

She assumed Daniel would get up then, relieve her of his warmth and weight. He didn't. He remained exactly where he was, his eyes narrowing in on her face, his gaze nearly palpable. It roamed across her cheeks, down her chin, and then settled on her lips. They tingled. Waiting for him to lean down and close the distance between them.

And how she wanted him to.

She should have been cold, half buried in snow. But she wasn't. He was like her own personal furnace. There was no reason to break the spell that was still stealing her breath.

His fingers grazed the line of her jaw, gently pinching her chin as his thumb slipped toward her lower lip. His own mouth opened a sliver, and his nostrils flared as he lowered his head.

Closing her eyes, she inhaled sharply, ready to savor the moment.

Suddenly Ruby's face flashed across the backs of her eyes, and reason rushed like icy water through her veins.

Ruby. Aretha. The plan.

Daniel wasn't hers to dream of or indulge in. He wasn't her heater or her protector. He wasn't hers. Period. End of statement.

Pushing him off, she jumped to her feet. She had no business thinking of him as her own personal *anything*. Not with Ruby in the picture. And especially not when she'd made a promise to Aretha.

thirteen

DANIEL COULDN'T SLEEP. He was also simultaneously too tired to keep his eyes open. The result was nearly losing his pinkie toe to the antique dresser in his guest room and a muted scream upon impact. Spitting out the cuff of his sweatshirt—which had been used to muffle said scream—he forced one eye open and stumbled into the hallway.

The Victorian two-story was dark, even the moonlight coming through the window at the end of the hall barely reaching inside. And aside from his own disruptions, the old lady sat silently.

Normal people weren't up at 4:30 in the morning. Normal people got more than a passing flutter of sleep.

Normal people could stop thinking about a certain someone's smile as she'd lain in the snow. They didn't constantly recall that tug low in the stomach. The one he hadn't felt in a very, very long time.

Normal people weren't consumed with a desire to kiss their favorite pastry chef just to know if she tasted as sweet as her pies. To know if she'd melt into them like pocket butter. To find out if her curls were softer than silk.

Coffee first. Then he'd come up with a plan for all the rest of that.

Because as long as Whitney was taking up all his waking moments—and forcing more of those than he wanted—he was going to have to do something about it.

He trotted down the hallway toward the back stairway, then held on to the handrail like the lifeline it was. His feet stumbled a few times, his socks falling off his toes and catching on the floorboards. As he jerked forward, his hand slid against the worn wood, but it held fast.

He owed a thank-you to whoever had double-bolted the wooden rail into the wall. Probably Seth.

He tucked that thought away as he arrived safely on the first floor, the kitchen dark and only the faint scent of yesterday's pies in the air. Scowling, he ran his hand along the wall, searching for a light switch. His middle finger connected with the side of a cabinet, and he grumbled again, pressing his sore knuckles to his lips. The whole house was out to get him.

After a long pause, he carefully stretched his fingers back to the cabinet and ran his hand along it until he reached the fridge. Around the door. Then to the hood over the stove. Three buttons there. He flipped one, and the fan turned on, angry and violent. It destroyed the silence, and he flung himself at the button to turn it off.

Quiet returned in an instant, and he held his breath as he tried the next one.

Light burned his eyes, and he stumbled backward into the corner of the island's countertop. It jabbed him in the hip as he swung his hands up to cover his face.

Maybe he'd have done better to stay in bed.

Memories of sledding with Whitney the day before were certainly preferable to bodily harm. The way she'd felt in his arms, trusting him enough to lean into him. To let him steer. The sound of her laughter, so infused with joy and delight. It had wound its way around his chest so many times that when they landed in the snowdrift, he hadn't been sure if it was Whitney or their dismount that had stolen his breath.

He should have rolled off her, held out his hand, and helped her up. Like a gentleman. His mom had drilled those reminders into his head for as long as he could remember.

Hold the door open for the lady behind you. Or in front of you.

Look people in the eye when you're speaking with them.

Speak clearly and don't mumble.

Help people up if they fall.

Don't lay on top of someone significantly smaller than you.

Okay, she hadn't said that last one. But she probably would have if she'd seen them in the snow.

He couldn't even blame his action—or lack thereof—on ignorance. He'd known better. But he hadn't been able to move for the rush of fire through his veins and the hammering of his heart, which had bounced against his ribs like a basketball, not in an attempt to escape but more of a reminder that it was there. That he hadn't been paying enough attention to it lately.

Then Whitney had smiled at him. And he wanted to kiss her.

God knew he hadn't wanted to kiss anyone since Lauren.

But the tug low in his stomach couldn't be denied. It was

like a rope tied to Whitney, connecting them, pulling him wherever she went.

He blinked hard against the light above the stove. It wasn't as bright as he'd thought, and his eyes quickly adjusted to the soft glow that stole across the tile countertops. The coffee maker sat in the corner, plugged in but empty. He set about fixing that, and within a few minutes, the heady aroma of dark roast filled the space, already clearing the fog from his mind.

He was a cup and a half and twenty minutes into daydreaming about Whitney when he realized he wasn't alone.

"You make enough of that to share?" Seth strolled over from the swinging door, rubbing his hand over his morning beard. His eyes, too, looked to be at half-mast, but he managed a dip of his chin in greeting.

Daniel offered a salute of his mug before taking another sip.

Seth poured himself a full mug, leaving no room for cream, and took a big gulp. "Mmm." He sighed into it as steam spirals rose. "Thanks. I usually have to make it when Caden's not here."

With a tip of his head, Daniel accepted the gratitude but said nothing else.

They stood in relative silence, only the occasional sips from their cups breaking the quiet. He didn't know much about Seth, but a man who could be still and silent was worth knowing.

Though Seth didn't keep it up for too long. "Hard time sleeping?"

Daniel glanced at his worn sweats and ran a hand through hair that was almost certainly a wild mess. "What gave it away?"

Seth chuckled. "I eventually ended up here too."

"At the inn?"

"In the kitchen." He flashed a partial grin. "I guess because I was looking for someone." His smile turned knowing.

"Marie?"

"Uh-huh. We spent a lot of hours here building this kitchen. Rebuilt it after it flooded too." Seth slurped a long sip. "You looking for Whitney?"

No. Maybe. "Yes."

He looked at his watch. "She'll be here soon."

As if on cue, the back door opened, the wind and cold howling through the mudroom and into the warmth of the kitchen. Feet stomped and Whitney's low voice hummed "Hark the Herald Angels Sing."

"Whoa." She paused midway through unwinding her scarf as she tumbled into the kitchen. "Wasn't expecting a welcoming committee. Did you bring muffins at least?"

Seth snorted, and Daniel easily found his own smile.

"Sorry, kid," Seth said as he put his empty cup in the sink and poured almost all of the carafe into a to-go bottle. "But I'll leave you a cup."

"So thoughtful." She laughed as he patted her shoulder and disappeared into the mudroom and beyond. Piling her coat and various cold weather accoutrements onto one of the island stools, she looked up. Her eyebrows jumped, almost like she was surprised to see Daniel still there.

"Morning." He raised his mug toward her. "I can make more if you want."

"You made the coffee?"

He nodded.

"Isn't it kind of early to be up and going?" She cocked her head, her gaze sweeping from his hair to his feet. "Well, *up*, anyway."

He gave himself a quick once-over too. There was no denying that he was still in his pajamas—in fact, he could feel the cool air coming through the hole under his arm. And he'd been too sleepy to bother with anything as trivial as a mirror when he'd left his room. Yeah, he probably looked like a mess compared to his normal. Compared to her.

Whitney looked like she had risen to summon the sun. Her honey-colored hair already glowed in the dim oven light, and her eyes shone like amber, warm and welcoming.

This was why he'd stumbled out of bed. He hadn't even known it then. But now he did. This was why he'd risked the stairs and the myriad other obstacles.

To see her.

With a shrug, he said only, "It's early for you too."

"Actually, I'm running a little bit late." She chuckled and marched toward the big stainless-steel refrigerator. "That is, if you want to eat breakfast and I want to get my pies made before the kids want to play."

"Need an extra pocket for your butter?"

She shot him a hard glare that melted faster than said butter in the microwave. "Not today. But you can do up the eggs." She paused, her eyebrows dipping with uncertainty. "You do know how to crack an egg, don't you?"

He snorted but put a hand to his chest in mock offense. "I—a confirmed bachelor—have never starved."

Her forehead wrinkled her disbelief at his performance.

"Okay, that's mostly due to takeout. But I know how to make eggs."

"Good." She held out a cardboard carton from the fridge. "Get to work. We need a dozen cracked and whisked in a bowl."

He stared at the carton for a long beat, trying to make

her think he hadn't yet decided if he was going to help her. Though that decision had been made the second the back door opened. He wasn't going anywhere.

Summoning as much dramatic flair as he could, he took the proffered eggs and began setting up a workstation beside the sink. "Bowl?"

From her place on the opposite side of the sink, she pointed a large knife at one of the top cabinets, then resumed cutting a slab of bacon. He thought she was wholly focused on her job as he reached for the plastic mixing bowl on the second shelf, but her loud snicker made him freeze.

When he looked down, she had craned her neck to get a better view of his armpit. "How long have you had that thing?" she asked.

"The sweatshirt? Since uni. So, ten years."

"No." She giggled again. "The hole."

He shrugged and returned to his spot. "Not quite as long."

"Why don't you fix it? I bet Marie has a sewing kit around here somewhere."

"And ruin the ventilation? I can wear this thing year-round. Warm in the winter. Cool in the summer. It's the perfect sweater."

"Or, you know, you could get clothes for each season."

"Why would I do that?"

She shook her head and laughed, her knife moving carefully over green onions and red peppers.

"You're really good at that, you know."

Her cheeks pinked, but she didn't look up from the smooth rocking motion of the knife as it skimmed past her knuckles.

The memory of their conversation on the night they'd looked at the lights came flooding back, and he blurted out his question before he could think twice. "Why don't you want to go to culinary school?"

The blade stopped mid-slice, but she didn't look up. "I already told you. I do want to go."

"But it's not your dream."

The corner of her bottom lip disappeared, and her eyes remained unblinking but also unfocused. He could tell she wasn't looking at breakfast. He just couldn't see what she did.

"Don't you have a dream?"

When she finally responded, her voice came out soft, as if from far away. "Do you?"

"I guess. I wanted to work in an office—to somehow use numbers."

"Why not a CEO? Why not start your own company?"

He snorted. "You have to be a people person for those roles. You have to be able to read other people and schmooze as needed and make small talk with people you don't know."

"You think Mark Zuckerberg is a people person?"

He focused on the egg in his hand, cracking it against the rim of the bowl. "I think Mark Zuckerberg had an idea and vision for something big enough that he doesn't have to play by the rules the rest of us do." He took a deep breath. "I like numbers. They don't require small talk. And they always work out. If they don't, I get to play detective and figure out why."

"Don't lie—did you want to be a cop when you were a kid? An investigator?"

"Not even a little bit. That job is messy. But we're not talking about me. We're talking about you and your dreams. Remember?"

She glanced at him out of the corner of her eye, her

mouth drawn into a tight line. "I want to have a dream." She stopped, her lips twitching as though she couldn't quite find the words. "You know in grade school when you'd have a project to research what you wanted to be when you grew up, and all the girls picked ballerinas and hairstylists and doctors? And the boys picked architects and baseball players and teachers? Well, I couldn't choose. So my dad suggested I look in the newspaper want ads to see who was hiring."

"What did you end up deciding on?"

"Sanitation worker."

He wanted to laugh. The very idea of pretty, petite Whitney driving a garbage truck and wrestling bins was absolutely ludicrous. But there was a sadness in her eyes that made him swallow his laughter and step closer to her.

"But you didn't choose that career path. You chose something better."

She shook her head until her hair danced. "No, I *settled* for something better. Not being able to decide," she whispered, "isn't the same as choosing."

He hadn't even realized he'd covered the four steps between them, but suddenly she was within arm's reach, and he ran his hand from her shoulder to her elbow, stopping there to squeeze gently. "You're a contradiction, Whitney. You tell me these stories, and I barely recognize the girl in them. You say you can't stick to anything, but then you put everything you have into going to a culinary school you don't really want to attend. And everyone in this inn loves you. You've clearly been showing up for Marie and Seth and Aretha and Jack for years. Marie and Seth trust you with their home and their kids. That means something."

"That's different."

"How?"

She blinked three times in quick succession before her gaze darted toward the window over the sink. He looked in the same direction toward the water beyond the field of glistening snow. The first rays of morning sun made everything sparkle.

"You've made this season special for those kids."

Whitney shook her head and stepped away. "I've been a mess. I don't have much planned, just whatever comes to mind."

"So what? They don't need an itinerary. They just need your time and your attention."

"But I'll say it again." She sighed. "It's not the same as having a dream."

"Then find one."

"It's not that easy."

He opened his mouth to push her a little more, to get her to reveal some truth that maybe she wasn't even telling herself. But she interrupted him.

"This isn't a therapy session. Now back to work and finish cracking the eggs so we can make the breakfast casserole."

"Already done. And no shell," he announced, double-checking just to make sure.

"Good job. Do you want a gold star?" She glanced at the paper taped to the far wall with Julia Mae's and Jack's names written on the left and a row of unevenly placed stickers following, each clearly celebrating their good behavior. At the end was written a prize for when they reached it.

Maybe he did want a gold star. Now he just had to figure out how to fill up a whole chart. Because the prize at the end would be Whitney. And he couldn't think of anything better.

fourteen

A COUPLE DAYS LATER, Whitney had just finished boxing the last pie of the morning when Aretha marched into the kitchen. Her eyes were focused and her lips tight as she plopped unceremoniously onto one of the island stools. It tipped to the side before righting itself with a clatter of wooden legs against hardwood floor.

"It's not working," Aretha huffed.

Whitney raised an eyebrow but hesitated to ask what she was referring to. In part because she needed to get the pies into the freezer at her place. And in part because she was afraid she knew the answer.

She'd been doing her best to keep her distance from Daniel. But the more she kept to the kitchen, the more he appeared there. Since the sledding incident, he'd stopped waiting for her to ask and began inviting himself into her domain.

She wasn't complaining that she'd arrived at the inn to find Daniel sipping coffee, hip against the counter, the last three mornings. Nor was she upset that he'd insisted on scrambling eggs while she fried up bacon and popped muffins into the oven. She wasn't even bothered by the way he'd sidled next to her at the stove, his breath warm on the back of her neck.

Nope. She was bothered by the way it didn't bother her. Not even a little bit. Not even at all.

Because it should.

Every minute he spent with her was time he wasn't spending with Ruby. Yes, she'd seen them sitting on the couch behind their spreadsheets more than once. But he was always so buttoned up. So prim and proper.

Ruby received the professional version of Daniel.

Whitney got the oversized sweatshirt with the hole and the uncombed hair. She got the laughter in his eyes and the rare chuckles he shared. She was on the inside of inside jokes. And she knew what it felt like to be held against his chest.

The Lord knew she wanted to feel that again.

Her cheeks flushed at the mere memory of their sledding excursion. She'd never felt quite so surrounded, quite so safe. She'd been terrified, but she'd also been certain that Daniel wouldn't let anything happen to her. That he was capable enough and that he cared enough.

And it made her bones feel like pudding.

Until she remembered Ruby.

Always she came back to Ruby.

While Aretha had offered to pay for the rest of her tuition, they'd never discussed what would happen if the plan failed. If Daniel and Ruby didn't find lasting love.

Whitney couldn't afford to find out. And she didn't dare ask. Maybe because she didn't really want to know. Or maybe because she couldn't let herself hope for it.

Aretha had been prattling away for several seconds, Whitney fully immersed in her thoughts of Daniel. When she blinked and caught the tail of Aretha's rant, she had no problem catching up. Because, of course, Aretha had been worried about her nephew's love life.

". . . just aren't spending enough time together. I hoped they'd go visit the quilters together, but Daniel seems intent on doing as much of that electronically as possible."

He'd also invited Whitney to go on any road trips they needed to take. Not that she was going to announce that to Aretha.

She didn't need any help looking like she was trying to get between the happy would-be couple. Which she was *not* doing. She was just stuck between . . . Daniel and his aunt's matchmaking scheme.

"We have to do *something*," Aretha implored, folding her hands beneath her chin.

Like leave them alone to let them figure it out on their own?

Whitney bit her tongue and attempted a smile. "Maybe they just need a little space."

Heaving a deep sigh, Aretha shook her head. "We don't have time for space. Christmas is right around the corner, and Ruby wants to finish up the acquisition so she can go home for the holidays. But if she goes home without Daniel, he'll be all alone."

Whitney sucked in a quick breath and choked out her surprise. "Isn't Daniel spending Christmas here?"

"Yes—but it would be so much better if they spent it together." Aretha batted her eyelashes, her gaze locked on somewhere far in the past. "My first Christmas with Jack was so romantic. Walking in the snow, holding hands along the boardwalk. Kissing under the—" Her eyes snapped into focus, her shoulders squaring. "The mistletoe!"

Whitney pressed a finger to her lips like she did regularly to hush the kids. "They're in the parlor," she whispered.

Aretha refused to be subdued. "That's perfect. We just need to call them out and then catch them in the doorframe."

She grabbed Whitney's wrist, dragging her toward the swinging door before she could formulate an excuse. And she needed an excuse. Anything. Because she did not think she could stomach watching Daniel and Ruby locked in a romantic embrace. No matter how much Aretha wanted to make it happen.

"But—but we need an excuse—I mean a reason—to call them."

Aretha paused for all of a split second. "Pie. Everyone comes running for pie."

"But won't they wonder why we didn't just bring it to them?"

"You're overthinking it." Aretha giggled, her cheeks already pink with delight. "This is going to be perfect."

Perfectly dreadful.

Whitney sucked in a breath and tried to force her heart to beat at a steady pace.

"Ruby!" Aretha called as soon as they stepped into the dining room. "Daniel! Come get some fresh pie."

Whitney jerked on her arm. "I don't have pie for them!" she hissed.

Waving off the concern, Aretha giggled behind her hand. "They'll forget all about the pie with a touch of the mistletoe magic."

"But what if they don't?"

"Well then, I'll buy one of the ones you just baked." Aretha didn't wait for agreement before hollering to her marks again. "It smells delicious! Come and get it." She paused in the middle of the dining room, her hands clasped beneath her chin and her gaze locked on the mistletoe.

The bulb of fake greenery glowed in the light of the afternoon sun shining through the window on the far wall, its bright red ribbons daring anyone to ignore the Christmas spirit.

"We'll be right there," Ruby called just as the front door swung open, ushering in a burst of cold air, Marie, and all three Sloan kids.

"Miss Whitney! Miss Whitney!" Jack ran toward her. "Amy has tonsillitis!"

He looked so pleased that she had to laugh, but she tried to cover it with her hand. When she finally pulled herself together, she squatted down in front of him. "Why are we so happy about Amy's illness? That's terrible."

"But now I get to be the angel," he announced.

"Ah. I see." She brushed his mop of thick brown hair. "I suppose you're going to need a halo."

"That does sound like cause to celebrate."

She looked up at the deep voice that had joined them. Daniel had walked through the parlor doorway and nearly into the foyer. His usual button-down and khakis had been replaced by a navy blue sweater that hugged his shoulders and made his eyes dance and jeans that looked as comfortable as they were worn-in.

There was no sign of Ruby.

Aretha's smile disappeared, her expression deflated and disappointed.

"So, where's this pie we were promised?" Daniel asked.

"Pie?" Julia Mae squealed and raced toward her mom's leg. "Can we have some? Please?"

"But you had a cookie after rehearsal."

Julia Mae's bottom lip pouted slightly. "But that was for being good during practice. This is to cel-brate."

Daniel let out an undeniable snort, and Whitney had to cover her mouth again to muffle more laughter. The kid had a point.

Marie shook her head and cupped her middle child's face with both hands. "All right. A *small* piece."

Julia Mae made a beeline for Aretha, grabbing her hand to tug her deeper into the maze of tables and toward the kitchen.

"You all sit down. I'll get the pie," Whitney said. "Let me just get Ruby." As she turned toward the parlor, Daniel shifted, and she collided with a sweater-covered shoulder. "Oops. Sorry," she mumbled, stumbling back.

Daniel caught her arm at the same time with a quick "Sorry about that."

Before she could move, Jack's voice rang out. "Look! You're under the mistletoe."

Whitney froze, not even needing to lift her gaze to know he was right. Her gaze stayed locked on Daniel's neck as he lifted his chin, his Adam's apple bobbing slowly, his jaw working back and forth a few times.

"Oooooh!" Julia Mae sang. "You have to kiss now."

Waving her hands in front of her, Whitney tried to step back, but Daniel still held her elbow, his grip firm and unmoving.

"Don't be silly," Aretha croaked. Whitney risked a glance across the room to find the older woman's complexion pale, the rosy tint to her cheeks erased. "That's just a ridiculous—"

Marie cut her off with a laugh. "It's tradition."

"Well, if it's tradition"—Daniel swallowed thickly—"we can't be the ones to break it."

"No. Nope. I don't—" Whitney tried to shimmy her way out from under the source of many a seasonal smooch. She didn't need to add herself to the list.

Not in front of the kids. And definitely not with Aretha looking on.

But there was something in Daniel's eyes that made her freeze. Maybe it was the way they dropped quickly then lifted back up to meet her gaze. Her lips tingled under the weight of his glance, and she had to return the favor. When her gaze settled onto his lips, she studied them. The comparative fullness of the bottom lip. The darker pink outline. The tiny upturn at the corners that was only for her. Only for someone studying them so carefully.

Her stomach took a full spin of delight. Then dropped swiftly in terror.

She gave him a quick shake of her head, but it was too late. His mouth was already forming the words she knew were coming.

"Is it okay if I kiss you now?" His hand on her arm squeezed tighter. Barely a perceptible change, but it was enough to send sparks shooting to the tips of her fingers.

Flexing her hands, she tried to shake them free of the tingling but ended up only twisting them into the softness of his sweater. Which he must have taken for agreement.

As any reasonable person would.

She hadn't meant it that way. She hadn't meant it as anything. It was just, he was steady, and she was flying apart from the inside out. And her hands had gotten lost in the fabric somewhere near the sides of his waist.

And he was leaning in.

Whitney sucked in a sharp breath and pinched her lips together, holding every single cell as tight as she could. She would just remain perfectly still, and no one would think anything of the kiss. And Daniel would surely understand that nothing should happen between them. That nothing was happening between them.

Yes.

Good plan. Remain completely stationary.

Then Daniel pressed his lips to hers.

They were warm at first. Gentle with firm pressure. And she almost sighed with relief. This wasn't anything special. It certainly wasn't what she'd imagined. Not that she'd been imagining what it would be like to kiss him. Much.

Then she did sigh. It wasn't loud or probably even noticeable. Except to Daniel.

He responded immediately, his hand slipping to her jaw. His thumb dragged from the corner of her mouth all the way to her ear as he tugged her closer.

Fire crackled in the wake of his touch, and she pressed into him, both the arsonist and the extinguisher. She was so consumed with finding some relief from the flames—and also finding more of them—that she relaxed her mouth.

The world disappeared. The inn and everyone in it vanished.

In a split second it was only the two of them. Only his lips on hers. The taste of hot cocoa and Christmas sugar cookies. The smell of pine and soap and something that was decidedly Daniel. The warmth of his body so near to hers.

Digging her fingers into his slim sides, she pressed in a little more, pulled him a little closer.

Suddenly his hand left her elbow and slipped around her back. His fingers spread between her shoulder blades. He sent shivers racing down her spine. She'd felt something similar in the snow and thought it was from the cold, thought she needed to go inside. But this . . . well, this was sweeter. Warmer. Entirely addictive.

Then his other hand slipped into the hair at the back of her head, his finger winding its way into a curl, tugging ever so gently.

"Ew! They're kissing!"

The inn and all its reality rushed back around them, swirling like a snow globe as Whitney jerked away from Daniel and tried to make sense of what had just happened. He didn't drop his hands, his fingers still pressing into her back, holding her close. And upright. She couldn't help but study his face, searching for some sign, confirmation of how he felt.

Oh, she knew he'd liked it. In the moment, he'd been so sweet. So tender. So certain.

But did he regret it? After?

He pressed his lips together for a moment as though testing them, making sure they were still there. Then the corners of his mouth ticked up ever so slightly. A smile just for her. Like his kiss had been. The tiniest promise that she need not worry.

She was the only one who would have regrets.

Tearing her gaze from his face, she spotted Ruby, arms crossed over her bright red sweater and a pout firmly in place on her matching lips.

"Well, what did you think was going to happen when you told them to kiss, silly?" Marie laughed at her little girl. "I think tradition has been safely upheld." Herding her kids toward the dining room, she said something sure to distract them all. "Come on. Let's get some pie."

Extricating herself from Daniel's embrace, Whitney raced into the kitchen, cheeks flaming, heart too big for her chest.

fifteen

"WHAT HAPPENED?"

Whitney grabbed the top pie, removed it from the pink box, and studied it as though it might rescue her from Aretha's interrogation.

"You were supposed to get Ruby and Daniel to kiss—not, you know, kiss him yourself."

"But I didn't kiss him," she argued. Technically correct. Perhaps splitting hairs, but she hadn't done the doing. He had started it.

Aretha's tilted head and fierce eyes said otherwise.

Turning to fully face her, Whitney took a deep breath. "I swear, I didn't mean for it to happen. And it didn't mean anything. It wasn't even a good kiss."

Aretha frowned, her hands finding her hips and her eyes narrowing as though she could detect a lie if she looked hard enough. "It didn't look like a bad kiss."

"We were just acting. Putting on a show."

Lord, forgive me for that lie. She had *not* been acting. She'd been consumed by him, whisked away into a holiday daydream better than she could have imagined. She'd fallen under a spell that made them the only two people on the planet.

The way he'd held her made her feel cherished.

Which was stupid. She'd known him for all of three weeks. And yet she'd also told him things she'd never told another soul. Things she wouldn't dare tell even her mom. They'd talked of dreams and futures, and she'd come close to telling him about that voice in her head. The one that shouted down every glimmer of direction, every hint of hope. The one that said she wasn't good enough and would never be.

She knew that voice too well. It had been on repeat for so many years.

Even now it told her that she'd messed up her only chance to go to culinary school. She'd ruined her only shot to make her dad proud. She couldn't make it through culinary school. She wouldn't ever be worthy.

But today there was a competing voice, a whisper, strong and bold. It sounded a lot like Daniel telling her that she was a stable friend. That she was doing her best. That there was a reason Marie and Seth trusted her and Caden had let her help in the inn's kitchen.

That maybe she hadn't ruined *everything*.

Blinking hard, she tried to focus on Aretha and what was coming out of her mouth.

"Acting?"

"We were just playing the part for the kids—just for a laugh. For tradition. But I didn't feel anything. And I'm absolutely certain he didn't either."

Except he might have. The way his whole body had trembled when she held on to his side . . .

Oh, she wanted to feel that again. She wanted to be the reason for that again.

"You're sure?"

She bit her tongue. "Mm-hmm."

A small shuffle on the other side of the swinging door made Aretha glance over her shoulder. Whitney followed the motion, but the door didn't move. She watched for shadows in the space at the bottom but didn't see any. Probably the kids eager for their pie.

When Aretha turned around, her voice dropped to little more than a breath. "But Ruby saw you."

"Maybe it made her a little jealous." At Aretha's worried expression, Whitney quickly added, "Though she has no reason to be."

"You're sure?"

"Positive."

Aretha finally looked appeased, and with a firm nod, she got out the plates and forks and helped Whitney dish up the dessert. When they carried it into the dining room, the excitement from the kids couldn't distract her from the conspicuously absent member of their party.

"Where's Daniel?" Aretha asked.

Marie looked up from her seat at one of the four-tops, her fork already halfway to her mouth. "I thought he went into the kitchen."

Jack shook his head, his mouth already full. "Wen' to the por'." Pointing toward the front door, he shoveled in another bite.

"I'll take this to him." Whitney held up the plate and refused to make eye contact with Aretha. Or Ruby.

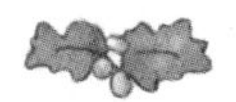

Daniel marched from one end of the porch to the other. Then he did it again. His feet refused to remain rooted. Not after what he'd overheard.

He shouldn't have been eavesdropping. He hadn't meant to. And he'd only heard a few words.

Just enough to ruin what he'd thought was turning into the perfect day.

He'd remembered to grab his jacket from the coat-tree before stepping outside, but the wind still whipped around him, chafing his ears and cheeks. He clapped his hands together, rubbing them briskly before shoving them into his pockets.

He should go back inside. And what? Face a woman who had thought their kiss was flat and meaningless?

Yeah, that sounded fun.

Blood roared through his ears, blocking out the splashing sounds of the bay, and heat rose from his forehead. He could have sworn . . . He'd been so sure that she felt . . .

He stomped a few more steps. Stopped and spun again. Then he kicked one of the Adirondack chairs, stubbing the same toe he'd nearly taken off a few days before. Pain throbbed all the way to his knee, and he wanted to scream.

Stupid. He was so stupid.

Lauren had always said he couldn't read people. His mom had said he had to try extra hard. Lauren said he could never try hard enough. It just wasn't in him. He was wired differently.

He'd basically laid his whole heart out for Whitney under that mistletoe, and she couldn't care less. Nothing. She'd said it meant *nothing*. That they'd been acting. That it wasn't even a good kiss.

Good? That kiss had been better than good. It wasn't great either. It blew all of those normal words out of the water. It was joy and hope and happiness rolled into one. It was strength and courage and the perfect pairing. She fit in his arms like she'd been born for that spot alone.

And he was happy to reserve it for her.

She'd smelled of cinnamon and sugar and the berries in her pies. She'd been warmer than a blanket on a cold night. And he'd held her so tight. Because she was where she belonged. And he belonged wherever she was.

True, he hadn't known her for very long, and he hadn't thought it possible to fall in love in such a short amount of time.

Until he met Whitney Garrett.

Or so he'd thought.

He stabbed his fingers through his hair, tugging on the top until it probably stood halfway to the roof. So what. He had no one to impress.

He was about to throw himself into one of the chairs—snow-covered though it was—when the red door swung open. Whitney peeked around the edge, a white plate outstretched.

He shoved his hands back into his hair and turned his back on the pie and the woman.

The door clicked closed, and he could feel her drawing closer, her warmth dividing the cold air.

"Are you angry with me?" Her voice was small, hesitant. "Did I do something wrong?"

Still with his back to her, he shook his head. "No. Go inside."

Out of the corner of his eye, he saw her set the pie on the table between the chairs, but she didn't walk away. Her breaths came out in a labored rhythm that was far too much like his own.

"Daniel. Talk to me. What did I . . . Should I not have kissed you?"

"Kiss me?" He spun around, a fire deep in his belly. "I'm

the one who kissed you, and apparently you didn't like it." He scrubbed his hand down his face, but he couldn't miss the wide-eyed shock on hers.

"What are you— What do you mean?"

"I heard you." He jabbed a finger in the general direction of the kitchen.

Her bottom lip disappeared beneath her front teeth. "What did you hear? Exactly."

"I heard you tell her it was just an act." He swallowed the bile that rose in the back of his throat. "I heard you tell her it wasn't even a good kiss."

"I'm—I'm sorry. I didn't mean for you to hear that." She pressed her hands to her cheeks, the pink there probably from her embarrassment rather than the wind.

"You didn't mean for me to hear it, or you didn't mean it?"

She shook her head, her features melting into what could only be called misery.

"That's not an answer."

"I know. I'm just so . . . I'm so sorry. Your aunt wants . . . that is, she wasn't very pleased . . ." Whitney huffed out a frustrated sigh when her tongue tripped over itself.

Only then did Daniel realize she wasn't wearing a coat over her blue and white knit sweater, and her shoulders twitched and shivered as she hugged herself.

His mother would never let him live it down if he didn't do something. He shrugged out of his jacket, wrapped it around her shoulders, and pulled it closed beneath her chin. And for a second, he thought she pressed the fabric to her nose and inhaled.

Ridiculous.

All of this was so implausible. But the only words he knew to explain it were already tumbling out of his mouth.

"The thing is, I'm not always great at understanding what people aren't saying. I can't always read between the lines. Shoot, sometimes I don't even know where the lines are. But I could have sworn that you liked that kiss as much as I did."

Her bottom lip trembled, and he reached for it, his thumb almost pressing to the plump center before he dropped his hand and turned his back to her again. It was easier to have a barrier between them. At least, it was easier not to have to look at her.

"My fiancée—I mean my ex-fiancée—she . . . she . . ." He sighed harshly.

"Lauren?"

He nodded, his chin falling to his chest as he dug a toe into a little mound of snow. "She was fond of reminding me that I didn't understand her. She accused me of not even trying most of the time. But I tried. I really did. I paid attention to all the little things, all the things she said I didn't care about. And maybe I didn't care about them as much as she did, but I cared about her. So I listened when she told me about her new throw pillows and the movies she wanted to see. Then I took her to see them. They were terrible—pretentious and pompous—but I sat through them. Paid for popcorn and soda and dinner after."

Memories of those dates with Lauren flashed through his mind, and he squeezed his eyes shut against the view of the street and the white slope down to the bay below. If he tried hard enough, maybe he could make his ex disappear too.

No such luck.

Lauren had left her mark. Her words still haunted him, made him doubt his emotions.

"Then she started pulling back. It was little things at first. Forgetting our anniversary or missing an appointment with the wedding cake woman. But I was paying attention. So I asked her what was going on. She promised me she was just distracted by so many moving parts of the wedding. She swore that she loved me and wanted to be my wife."

A small hand pressed to the center of his back. "What happened?"

"Exactly what you think."

"I couldn't guess."

His shoulders sagged as he looked up. "She felt so distant. Even when we were together, she was somewhere else. It was like she stopped focusing on me. Like she couldn't see me anymore. We were having dinner one night, and she looked right through me. So I asked her what was going on, point-blank. She told me I was imagining it all. She said I would have been just as distracted if I was juggling all the wedding details. Everything would be fine once we were married.

"I felt like I was losing my mind, like I couldn't trust what my eyes were telling me. My ears heard what she said, but my eyes saw something else. And I couldn't figure out which of my senses to trust."

He choked back something that sounded suspiciously like a sob—though it couldn't be. He hadn't cried over Lauren. Maybe ever. But admitting the pain and confusion of those months to Whitney brought back every stab of regret straight to the center of his chest.

"Lauren had spent years telling me that I couldn't trust myself. So when she kissed me that night, I thought I had to be wrong. Obviously, she loved me. She was planning our wedding."

"But there was no wedding."

"No."

Suddenly her hand disappeared from his back, replaced by

her forehead at his shoulder and her arms slipping around his waist. She held him, firm and reassuring, as though she could make him forget all the pain that Lauren had caused. Her embrace gave him the confidence to tell her the rest.

"I found out a week before we were supposed to be married."

"Found out?"

"Lauren had been seeing her poetry professor. Rumor had it, it was nothing serious. Well, not to anybody but me." He cleared his throat. "She told me she wanted someone who could feel something, and she didn't think I could."

"Oh, Daniel." Her words sounded kind, but he worried they were really patronizing instead.

"I don't want your pity. I just need your honesty." He held his breath as he tried to form the truth on his tongue. "I need to know that I am not imagining things. That you felt something when we kissed. Like I did."

sixteen

THE WAITING WAS HARDER than Daniel had expected. Perhaps it was harder even than putting the truth out there. He couldn't see Whitney, could only feel her burrowed into his back. Her hands had been swallowed by the sleeves of his jacket, but her hold was tight enough to give him hope.

Her silence was loud enough to give him pause.

The cold air sliced through him, and a shiver racked his whole body. Still, he waited.

Finally, she sucked in a quiet breath. "I'm sorry."

That did not answer his question. Unless . . . "Sorry about what happened with Lauren? Sorry that you didn't like the kiss? Sorry that you got caught under the mistletoe with me at all?"

Instead of speaking, she rubbed her cheek against his back. It felt a little like a big cat pressing into him, and he wanted to turn around to see her face. But first he needed an answer. A real one.

"I'm sorry," she said again, her repeated words emptying whatever hope he'd let himself find. "I'm sorry that Lauren couldn't see you for who you really are."

He jerked with the force of her resolve, everything inside him going rigid.

"I'm sorry that she treated you so badly. If you ever kissed her like you kissed me today, she was the fool. Not you. And I'm sorry that I lied to Aretha."

He spun in her arms and she let out a peep of surprise, but he wrapped himself around her, barring any chance of her escape until she said more. He wanted all of those words, all of that sentiment. They made his blood pound in his veins and his heart feel too big for his ribs.

Whitney kept her gaze down, a sheepish smile tugging at her lips, so he dipped down until he could look into her eyes. "You lied to my aunt?"

"Um . . . well, I may not have been fully honest with her."

"How 'not fully' are we talking here? Was it a little white lie? Or a full-blown deception?"

Her neck turned red, and she pressed her face into his shoulder so he couldn't see her. Her whole body trembled, and he slipped one hand up her back, beneath his jacket and over her sweater. She was warm and inviting. With his other hand, he cupped the back of her head, combing his fingers into those beautiful curls.

He held her until she was ready to speak, until he'd proven that he was safe.

"It was definitely the latter," she said, her breath warming his collarbone.

"But why?"

She paused again, burrowing deeper. A low hum from the back of her throat preceded her next confession. "Because I was surprised by how much I felt. Because I didn't want to admit it to Aretha." She swallowed audibly. "Or myself."

He wanted to pump his fist in the air and crow like a

rooster. Not an urge he'd had before. Then again, Whitney had never admitted that she'd thoroughly enjoyed their kiss before either.

But she had.

He hadn't imagined it or misread the situation. He hadn't fabricated her response in the depths of his mind.

And if she'd enjoyed it as he had, she probably wanted more too.

Crooking a knuckle beneath her chin, he tilted her face toward him. Her eyes glowed as she seemed to fight a smile. That was all the encouragement he needed.

Leaning in, he kissed her softly.

"Eep." Her giggle overflowed with nerves. "Sorry."

"Do you not want to?"

"No, it's just that your aunt . . ."

He didn't need to hear another word about Aretha. He only needed to hear that Whitney was right where she wanted to be.

He kissed her again. No hesitation or worry or second-guessing. No audience or interruptions. Only the two of them. And her lips.

They were soft and yielding and tasted like the coffee she made most mornings. He'd expected a hint of her boysenberry pie there, but apparently she hadn't eaten any either. Which was fine with him. She was plenty sweet without it.

She fisted her fingers into the front of his shirt, pulling him closer and closer until there was nothing between them but the breaths they stole in order to keep going.

His heart thudded almost from outside him. It was so loud that she had to be able to hear it too. Or maybe that was hers thundering against him. He couldn't tell where he stopped and she started, so he wound his arms tighter. She melted into him, all softness and light, heat and joy.

This was what it felt like to hold the morning sun.

Go ahead and try to tell him he didn't have feelings.

He knew it was a lie now because Whitney made him feel things that he'd never even thought possible. Her small hands wound into his sweater told him he belonged. The soft sigh that escaped her lips promised that he could bring joy. And with the giving came a healthy dose of receiving.

They said it was better to give than to receive, and he was sure that applied to this situation. Because the more he gave, the more his own heart swelled. Never had he understood the Grinch's plight so well as he did in that moment. His heart had absolutely grown three sizes.

He was full, brimming with a happiness that he'd never dared to hope for, waiting for it to spill over. But it never did. He just kept growing fuller and fuller until he thought he'd burst. Then somehow he found more room for it—his heart found a new capacity for joy.

Whitney finally pulled back, her ragged breaths tearing between them, eyes wild, and a smile wider than the ocean splitting her face. "That was—" She paused to suck in another breath, her shoulders rising and falling dramatically.

"Yeah. I know." He laughed.

She chuckled as she reached toward his face. Her hand was still consumed by his jacket, but she wrestled her fingers free, finally touching the corner of his mouth. "I should have known."

"Hmm?" He couldn't risk forming a question that would make her pull away.

"You have the best smile. That's why you were hiding it. You were afraid all the girls would fall for you."

He didn't hold back his laugh then. Nor his response. "Unlikely."

Thank goodness she didn't pull away. Her fingers combed along the short stubble across his jawline.

"I just didn't know I had a reason to use it."

If it was possible, her smile gleamed even brighter, her whole face lit up like Mr. Huntington's home. "You do now. I promise."

All those Christmas songs and sappy holiday movies—this was what they were about. He hadn't thought it was real, but now joy was standing in his arms.

Whitney dropped another egg and could do nothing but watch it splatter across the floor. Perfect. She'd just needed the butter from the back of the fridge, but now she had another mess to clean up. At this rate, every pie she sold at the next market would only cover the cost of wasted materials.

She could forget about making her tuition payment. Even with Aretha's help.

Her stomach spasmed in a painful cramp at the very thought of the older woman, and she leaned against the edge of the counter as though it might offer some relief. It did not. It couldn't. No inanimate object was going to make her feel better about ruining Aretha's plan and not telling her the truth.

And there was no way around that. No amount of icing or crumb topping could make the reality any less than ruination.

Aretha had had a plan for her nephew's joy and good. For a long-term relationship and a family and the whole thing.

And Whitney had stepped right into the middle of it.

She had no idea what exactly was happening between her

and Daniel, but she couldn't be counted on to stick with anything. Except maybe . . .

Daniel had said she stuck by people. She'd tried a hundred different activities but kept the friends she'd known since high school. Maybe it was possible her relationships could last.

Though she'd begged Daniel not to tell his aunt about their budding whatever-it-was—and he'd agreed—Aretha was eventually going to find out. Moreover, she was going to know that Daniel and Ruby hadn't gotten together.

Whitney dumped a cup of brown sugar into the bowl on the counter. Then she looked at it closer. Was that the first cup or the second? Or an accidental third? The clumps of packed sugar broke apart, sliding down the mound and filling the bowl until she couldn't even see the flour at the base.

And she had added the flour. She was sure. Well, pretty sure.

But what about the cinnamon and nutmeg?

There was a good chance this was going to be the worst crumb topping ever made.

She had no one to blame but herself. She'd much rather be distracted by Daniel and that kiss—both kisses, for that matter. But no . . .

She scowled at her mixing bowl, then at the sugar canister. She'd almost certainly added an extra cup. If she did a recipe and a half, the ratios would be right, and the pies would have some extra topping. It was everyone's favorite part anyway.

She reached for the flour, dug her measuring cup in, and tried to focus on the recipe. Not on what she was going to say to Aretha when the truth came out.

"Hey, Whitney!"

Her whole body jumped, including the arm holding the

canister. It slipped from her grasp, then in slow motion, it hit the floorboards and a cloud of white exploded to her waist, coating her apron and all the uncovered parts of her black leggings.

Laughter burst from the back hall that led to the office, and she looked up, a strange burning at the backs of her eyes.

Marie leaned against the doorframe, her hands covering her mouth and her eyes squinting in glee. "I'm so sorry. I didn't mean to surprise you."

"You didn't." She looked down at the clear evidence to the contrary. "I mean, you did. But it's okay."

Only it suddenly didn't feel okay. It all felt like too much. Instead of tiptoeing for the broom and beginning the task of cleaning up, she sagged against the counter and then slid down the lower cabinets, pressing her hands to her face as she curled over her bent knees.

"Hey. Hey. It's okay. We'll get it cleaned up." An arm slipped across her shoulders, and Marie's voice was right next to her ear.

"It was my fault. I'll—" Her voice cracked, and she somehow felt lower. She hadn't thought that was possible. But the knot that had been twisting tighter and tighter all morning suddenly snapped, releasing a rush of tears that leaked down her cheeks no matter how fast she blinked or how hard she sniffed.

"Whitney. Honey? What's wrong?"

"Nothing. I'm fine. It's fine. Everything's fine."

Marie pressed into her shoulder. "Obviously not. Unless those are happy tears."

Whitney hiccuped—quite unceremoniously—and shook her head.

"I didn't think so. So tell me what's going on."

"You probably have to get to the church. Don't you have some pageant things to work on?"

"Yes. But they'll wait. What has you so torn up?" Marie squeezed her arm. "I thought—well, I thought that you had a bit of mistletoe magic after you and Daniel . . . you know."

"Kissed in front of everyone?" She hadn't expected her voice to sound so frosty, but there it was. When Marie didn't say anything, she peeked out between her fingers. "I'm sorry."

Marie's eyes narrowed, the weight of her gaze heavy. "I thought you liked Daniel. I thought you were maybe falling a little bit for him."

Oh dear. If she'd been so transparent that even Marie, with everything on her plate, had noticed, Aretha was sure to see it too.

"I do like him," she whispered.

"So, what's the problem? It's clear to anyone with eyes that he adores you."

Whitney nibbled on her lip. He did like her. He'd told her as much. But the secrets and lies were eating her up.

"It's just . . . Aretha."

The tip of Marie's nose wrinkled in concern. "I don't understand. Aretha loves you too. Do you think she wouldn't approve?"

Pressing her hands to the tumbling in her stomach, Whitney hung her head. "Aretha has . . . other plans for Daniel."

"You mean with Ruby?"

Whitney managed a quick nod.

"I thought she'd given up on that idea. I figured she'd seen the truth." With a laugh, Marie leaned her head back against a white cabinet drawer. "Ruby is way too serious for him. He needs someone to bring some balance to his life, not someone who adds more pressure. He needs someone like you."

Warmth seeped through her chest, spreading wider with every beat of her heart. She wanted to hug Marie for saying such a lovely thing.

"But that's not all."

"Tell me."

"Promise you won't tell a soul? Not even Seth."

Marie pressed her lips into a tight line but gave a decisive nod.

"You know how Aretha asked me to help her set them up?"

"Go on."

She didn't want to admit that she'd been so easily convinced to help with the promise of a little bit of money, but there wasn't a way around that truth. "It's just that my dad thinks I can't follow through on anything."

"Well, that's not true. But what does your dad have to do with Aretha's plan?"

She peeked at Marie out of the corner of her eye before brushing flour from her leggings. It only seemed to spread the white wider. "I've tried a hundred things, and every time it gets a little hard, I find a reason to give up. My dad said he wasn't going to bail me out again. And I'm so close to the culinary school, but I'm not going to make enough to pay my tuition and hold my spot."

Marie leaned closer. "I still don't understand what that has to do with Aretha and Daniel."

Pinching her eyes closed and sucking in a steadying breath, Whitney released it all. "Aretha said she'd make up the difference to cover my tuition if I made sure Daniel and Ruby got together."

"She. Did. Not." Marie swung away, then back, her eyes

wild with fire. "That meddling old biddy. I love that woman like family, but how dare she?"

"No, it's my fault."

"You didn't have another choice."

"Yes, I did. And I should have turned her down."

Marie jumped to her feet and brushed her white hands across her pants, leaving a trail of flour in her wake. Whitney scrambled to join her, much less graceful but still managing to get in Marie's way before she could march to the shop.

"I'm going to give her a piece of my mind."

"You can't!" Whitney tugged on her arm. "Please don't. You promised."

Marie paused mid-stride. Her eyes still flashed with determination, but a bit of steel leaked from her tiny shoulders. "You're clearly upset about this, and Aretha is holding you hostage with the promise of what? A few thousand dollars?"

She shrugged a general agreement.

"It's not right. You're the one who made Daniel smile. That man's facial muscles had atrophied until you reached him."

But for good reason. Anyone who knew what Lauren had done wouldn't have begrudged him his grumpy ways. Though admittedly she much preferred his smile to his scowl. And since their second kiss, those full grins were more common.

"It's not Ruby who makes his eyes shine. Or bakes him pies."

Well, technically Whitney hadn't baked a pie specifically for him either. But he sure had enjoyed sampling the ones she wasn't sure if she'd destroyed.

"Aretha is a fool if she thinks Ruby is the right fit for him. And I don't mind telling her as much. Family tells each other the truth."

"Please don't," Whitney begged. "I'll talk with her. I'll tell her I can't go through with it."

Marie looked unconvinced but finally said, "All right. But hear this, Whitney. Daniel would be lucky to have you."

That would have been a lot easier to believe if she hadn't been part of Aretha's plan from the beginning.

seventeen

"COME ON, COME ON, COME ON. Zip up your coats and put on your scarves."

Daniel felt the call almost as urgently as Whitney's charges, and he poked his head out of the dining room to find the trio bundling up near the front door. Whitney squatted in front of little Jessie, closing her coat and popping her little hands into mittens before checking on the other kids.

"Where ya going?" he asked.

Jack looked up from the end of his zipper, which refused to stay in place. "I have rehearsal, and then we're going to look at the lights again."

"Wanna come with us?" Julia Mae asked. "I have to sit really quiet by myself 'cause Miss Whitney has to help Jack with his costume."

Good luck with that. He caught Whitney's eye and immediately recognized the same concern there. But she smiled up at him and responded with a wink.

As he knelt beside her on the entry rug, he reached for Jack's delinquent zipper. "Sounds fun."

"Oh, really?" Whitney raised an eyebrow that suggested he wasn't telling the truth.

But any time with her sounded fun. They only had a week until Christmas, and he wanted to spend as many of those days with her as possible. "Let me turn off my computer," he said with a nod toward the dining room.

"And change your clothes?" she said, but then she did a quick double take.

He swept his hand down his new sweater and motioned to his new jeans—ones he hadn't even had to borrow.

"Where's your school uniform, Mr. Daniel?" Jack asked.

He chuckled. "School uniform?"

"Yeah." Julia Mae nodded as Whitney wound a scarf around her neck. "Jack wears a blue shirt and brown pants to school too."

Whitney snorted at that. "Mr. Daniel isn't in school anymore. He gets to pick what he wears."

"But why would you wear the same thing every day if you get to pick?" Jack asked, his eyes as big as saucers.

"Good question, little man," Daniel said as he pushed himself to his feet. He didn't have much of an answer, so he told the truth. "I guess I never spent time thinking about it."

At the same moment, Whitney said, "His blue shirts make his eyes pop."

"They do?"

A lovely blush spread over her cheeks and probably reached her ears, which were hidden by her hair. "Yes."

"Maybe I should keep wearing them."

Whitney met his gaze and whispered, "Maybe you could find a sweater in that same blue."

"Ew! Are you going to kiss again?" Jack spat the words out as if they tasted like dirt.

If Daniel had any say in it, the answer was a resounding yes.

Whitney giggled and shooed them toward the door. "We have to leave now or we'll be late. But catch up to us?"

He made quick work of sending one more email, closing his laptop, and pulling on his shoes. His jacket was still in his hands when he slammed the door behind him and raced down the steps to the boardwalk. The wind off the water sliced through him, but he pressed into it as he slid his arms into the sleeves. Zipping up his coat seemed to just close the cold in with him, but it was worth it the moment he spotted Whitney with Jessie on her hip and two bouncing balls leading the way.

Someone had shoveled the boardwalk, but the gray wood blended into the little mounds on either side. He prayed there weren't invisible patches of ice as he picked up his speed. His lungs pumped out regular puffs of air as he caught up with them.

"That was fast," Whitney said.

He brushed a hand against the small of her back, and her eyes flashed with something that looked like joy. And for a split second he could picture their future. Quiet strolls in the evening light. Holding hands just because. And children.

Her children.

His.

Theirs.

His future that had been nothing but work suddenly felt full, and his heart skipped a beat. It wasn't the dream that filled him. It was Whitney—her light. It was the way he could close his eyes and still see it shining through the darkness.

He pressed his lips to her cheek. It was chilly but immediately turned even more pink.

"Daniel." She swatted his arm. "Not in front of the kids."

But Jack and Julia Mae happily trotted several paces ahead of them, their focus on jumping into the patches of light from the old-fashioned iron streetlamps.

"They wouldn't notice if I kissed you full on the lips."

Her eyes went wide.

"Which I'd like to do, by the way."

She swallowed thickly, her gaze dropping until it stopped at his lips. Good. She was thinking about it too. Probably not as often as he was. But he'd take whatever she could give him.

She shook her head. "Not here. Not now." But she slipped her arm into the crook of his, falling into stride beside him. And he enjoyed every step up to the church building.

At the front door, he paused. He hadn't been inside one since . . . since he was supposed to get married in one. Strange. He'd thought it would bring a flash of regret. But when Jack wrenched the big wooden door open, the warmth inside beckoned to him.

From the far back corner, a piano pumped out the chorus of "Away in a Manger," soft voices humming along.

He followed the others inside and paused, the closed door at his back. The sanctuary wasn't overly large—two rows of wooden pews fourteen deep. On the end of each bench, along the center aisle, hung a small green wreath with alternating red and white bows. An upright piano sat on the corner of the stage that dominated the front of the room. Partially hidden by the piano, a twelve-foot fir tree had been professionally decorated in silver and red. It didn't suffer from the same overdecorating that the kids had bestowed on the inn's tree.

On the opposite side of the stage, a cardboard cutout of a stable sat among a haphazard spread of real straw. It didn't have the brilliance of Mr. Huntington's barn scene, but it left no doubt about what—or rather who—took center stage in their pageant.

Above it all, a cross hung, its beams made of rough-hewn logs. There was nothing clean or precise about it, but he couldn't seem to look away.

"Come on, Mr. Daniel." Julia Mae tugged on his hand, pulling him from his inspection. Whitney, Jessie, and Jack were already halfway down one of the side aisles. Marie met up with them, reaching for Jessie and hugging her close as she pointed Jack toward a door to the side of the stage. He and Whitney quickly disappeared.

In a move far too much like an adult, Julia Mae pointed to the back pew. "Sit here."

"All right." He slid along wood smoothed by years of churchgoers, and Julia Mae clambered up beside him. "Do you want to take off your jacket?" he asked as he unzipped his own.

"No. I want to be ready when it's time to go." She pursed her lips to the side. "But maybe I could take my mittens off. They're attached." She showed him the string that connected the buttons from her cuff to her homemade mittens.

"Sound planning."

Julia Mae sat on the very edge of the bench, leaning forward as a dozen kids began filing onto the stage, her feet swinging with endless energy. Out of nowhere her little voice broke the silence. "You're not lonely anymore, are you, Mr. Daniel?"

He jumped at the whispered words. They were spoken more toward her knees than to him, but they still packed a wallop. The swish-swish of her snow pants didn't stop as she bobbed her curly head in time to the Christmas carol floating from the piano and the youthful voices adding the lyrics.

Clearing his throat, Daniel tried to make sense of what she'd said. "What makes you say that?"

Tilting her head, she looked up at him through squinting eyes. The narrow slits somehow made the blue even more vibrant, more intense. And he wondered if a four-year-old could read his mind.

She'd laugh if she knew he'd just been thinking about her nanny.

Julia Mae smacked her little lips. "'Cause. You don't look like Eeyore anymore."

Holding up his hands, he wiggled his fingers in front of her face. "I was thinking I never did. I've never been gray, as far as I know. And I don't have a tail. Not even a lost one."

"Mr. Daniel." She giggled. "Not like that. Like there." She waved a hand in his general direction.

"Like where exactly?" He suddenly needed to know what she meant.

She hopped up on the wooden seat, knelt next to him, and clamped her little hands on either side of his face. The mittens swinging from their ties bounced against his shoulders as she squeezed only hard enough to keep his attention. Then one hand moved, and she pressed the cool pad of her finger against the line next to his mouth. "Right here." Her finger moved to the space between his eyebrows. "And here." She squinted harder at a spot below his nose, finally pressing against the center of his scruffy mustache. "Here too."

He couldn't help the rise of his eyebrows and didn't have any words to follow her proclamation.

Clearly Julia Mae didn't need him to. She flipped around, plopped back down on the pew, and proclaimed, "And I know why."

His stomach did a full loop. He'd promised Whitney he

wouldn't say anything. For whatever reason, she wasn't ready for the inn's residents to know, and he'd much rather have her and a secret than neither.

It wasn't possible the little girl—precocious as she was—had clued in to their budding relationship. Was it?

"It's 'cause it's Christmas."

"Huh?"

"'Cause of Mam-nuel."

He nearly choked on a cough. "I'm sorry, what?"

"Mam-nuel. My daddy told me all about him."

Daniel leaned forward to watch her face, to see if she was teasing him. But there were no signs that she was anything but earnest.

"Mam-nuel?" He tried it out on his tongue, but it still didn't make sense.

Julia Mae rolled her eyes like he was clearly out of the loop. "You know. When Jesus was born in the manger. God came to be with us."

"Emmanuel."

The word came out so loud that the pianist hit a sour note, and every pint-size head on the stage swiveled in his direction. Even Whitney shot him a sideways look from the wings.

He held up his hands and mouthed a quick apology as the choir found their place and fell back into the carol's verse.

Turning back to Julia Mae, he whispered, "Emmanuel?"

"That's what I said." Making her mittens dance like a marionette, she didn't bother looking in his direction again. "My daddy said that God didn't want us to be alone, so he sent Ee-man-ee-al."

He smiled at her exaggerated pronunciation efforts. Or maybe it was the truth of her words.

"You're not lonely because God's with you, right?"

Daniel tried to croak out an agreement, but the truth wasn't so easy. Honestly, he'd decided God had given up on him years ago. Right about the time Lauren had walked out the door. About the same time he'd decided she might be right that he didn't know how to feel anything.

His gut twisted at the memory, which was almost immediately replaced by the sure knowledge that he had feelings. Big ones. For Whitney.

A tiny hand pressed on his thigh right above his knee. "Mr. Daniel? That's why, right? 'Cause you're not alone."

Slowly he nodded, swallowing against a lump that had found purchase in the back of his throat.

He'd been alone for so long that he'd almost forgotten what it meant that God loved him. That God could be *with* him. That God loved to give good gifts.

Maybe Julia Mae was right. Those gifts felt a lot like walking beside Whitney.

eighteen

WHITNEY WAS GOING to tell Aretha the truth. She didn't know how or when. But after ruining *another* pie crust, she couldn't afford not to.

And then she would tell Daniel. She just needed to find a moment with him. Alone. A moment where Aretha wasn't still pushing him and Ruby together. The two business gurus had been busy finalizing agreements with the quilters, and Aretha had hovered over them like a mother hen.

But the moment she could get Aretha by herself, the lies had to end. And with them, hopefully her sleepless nights would too.

Her hand brushed over the sharp corner of the envelope sticking out of her apron pocket. Ignoring the twist of her stomach at the reminder, she rubbed her eyes with the heels of her hands and focused on the fresh peaches swimming before her. If she messed up now, she was liable to lose a finger, not just have a soggy pie crust. She cut through the fruit's flesh with slow, steady movements. Then she turned the peach half and sliced it at a ninety-degree angle.

She had only one farmers' market of the season left, and only a handful of pies yet to bake.

Not that it mattered. She wasn't going to culinary school. She couldn't take Aretha's money—even if by some miracle Aretha still offered it. And she couldn't make the tuition without it.

At this point—after she broke Aretha's heart and then Daniel's—she didn't think she'd have much desire to attend anyway. Mostly, she wanted to disappear. Before she had to come clean with them all if possible.

But that wasn't how these things worked. She'd much prefer to bail as soon as it got hard. Like soccer. Like fiddle. Like swimming.

Yet these were people's lives she was dealing with. This wasn't a flying ball to the face without any feelings of its own. These were people who deserved the truth—even if it hurt her to say it.

She needed the Lord's strength because she was about to set her whole Christmas season on fire.

"There you are!"

Whitney spun at Daniel's voice, facing him down, knife outstretched before her.

"Whoa!" He chuckled, hands held up in surrender.

"Sorry." She dropped the knife to the cutting board and scooped her peach bites into a mixing bowl.

"Hey, are you all right?"

"Fine."

Uncertainty was clearly spelled out across the pinched line of his eyebrows, and she knew it wasn't fair to make him doubt his interpretation of her response. Not when he was right.

"I'm just up in my own head today. I'm sorry. It's not you." *It's me.*

His warm hand slipped across the small of her back, a little bit possessive, completely sweet. It said she belonged *with* him. And he with her. She couldn't help the way her head fell back and into his shoulder. Just for a second she closed her eyes, and the voice that had been screaming at her for days drew silent.

He pressed his lips to the side of her forehead, and the ache that had been her constant companion eased.

"You look pretty today."

"Don't say that. I look like a mess." No mirror was required to know that her hair had turned frizzy and her cheeks were dusted with flour from the remade crust.

He brushed her hair from her forehead, dragged a finger down to her chin, then pressed his thumb ever so gently to her lips. "I don't see any mess at all."

Great. Now she was going to turn into a puddle. "You can't just say things like that."

"Says who?"

What if someone heard? What if he knew the truth? He would hate himself for believing even for a minute that she was something she wasn't.

Like a snap of her fingers, the voice was back, and she pushed away from Daniel's warmth. "I have to get these pies done before the market on the twenty-second."

"Great. I'll help you—and maybe you can help me?"

She sprinkled sugar over the cut peaches. "What do you need help with?"

"A ride to Georgetown."

"You're not cheating on my pies with the goodies at the Maroon Pig, are you?" The little bakery along the southeastern coastline was island famous for their rhubarb cinnamon rolls, but to her, their butterscotch brownies were as close to a taste of heaven as she'd find this side of eternity.

He chuckled, that shallow dimple teasing her. "Never. But we have one quilter who doesn't do computers. Or the internet. She asked us to fax her the agreement."

Whitney cringed. "Does anyone actually own a fax machine anymore?"

"Poppy Donaldson in Georgetown, apparently."

She snorted. "No, she doesn't."

"Probably not personally, but maybe. The problem is we don't have a fax machine on this side to send it from. And the back and forth on a fax machine will just drag it out. Ruby and I agreed that a trip to see Poppy in person is a much better idea. Otherwise, we'll never get this wrapped up before Christmas." He nudged her shoulder with his. "What do you say? Up for a road trip?"

"Just the two of us?" She didn't know if she sounded hopeful or not. She wasn't even sure if she was. Uninterrupted time alone with him meant she'd have to make good on the promise she'd made to herself.

"Um, and Ruby."

She sighed louder than she'd expected. Relieved that she wouldn't have to tell him the truth just yet.

Because she was a coward.

"Yeah. I can do that." It wasn't like she had to bake pies anyway. It didn't really matter how many she took to the market.

"Great!" He pressed a quick kiss to her lips. "Now, put me to work."

"You're sure?"

"Everything for Aunt Aretha is done—except for Poppy's signature. The sale is going to be completed right after the

New Year, and I just want to spend the afternoon with my favorite girl."

"You still can't say things like that." But she knew her smile took the legs out from under her argument. "Come on, let's get you cleaned up." When she lifted her apron to wipe her hands, the white envelope it had been storing flopped to the floor.

"What's this?" Daniel stooped and picked it up, studying the return address. "From the culinary institute? Why haven't you opened it?"

She studied the floral pattern of the fabric between her fingers for a long moment. "It's a last call to pay the tuition or lose my spot."

"How do you know?"

"Because the previous three emails said I'd get a final written notice."

The line of his jaw worked back and forth. "So, pay the tuition."

He made it sound so easy, so black-and-white. She wished it could be. "I'm not going to go."

Jerking back as though she'd slapped him, he said, "I don't understand. This was your plan."

"But not my dream. Haven't you been reminding me of that for weeks?" She tried for a smile, but it fell flat.

"Have you figured out your dream?"

"No." She shrugged. "I was never going to make it to culinary school. I can't commit to anything, right?"

"Whitney? Talk to me. What's going on?"

The words were on the tip of her tongue, ready to spill out. The truth of what she never should have agreed to.

But instead, a different truth poured out.

"It's what I do. It's what I've always done. I give up when things get difficult."

He shook his head, and she wasn't sure if it was because he didn't understand or because he didn't agree. If the latter, she could prove it to him.

"The only dream I've ever had was to be a dolphin trainer."

"A lot of call for that on the island?"

She shoved his shoulder. "I'm serious. I was seven, and I'd seen a show about a dolphin, and someone told me it was someone's job to train that dolphin. And I wanted to do it. They seemed so smart and were so sleek in the water. The kids in my class told me it was a stupid dream. No one from little North Rustico would ever work with dolphins."

"What do kids know?"

"That's what I said. So I kept at it, reading all about dolphins, learning how they're trained."

He nodded thoughtfully. "Sounds smart. And then you studied marine biology?"

"No. I didn't get that far. I got to the pool and nearly drowned on my first day of swimming lessons. Like, the lifeguard had to rescue me. And they took me to the hospital in an ambulance."

He grabbed her hand, pressing his fingers to her wrist as though to confirm that blood still pumped through her veins and she had survived the ordeal.

"I lived." She did a little jig to prove it—like her chattering wasn't evidence enough.

His grin was worth it.

"When my mom came to get me at the hospital, she was . . . well, I think she was relieved. But she was furious. I wanted to get back in the water and learn to swim. I couldn't swim with dolphins if I couldn't *swim*, if I was afraid of the water. But she forbade me from setting foot on a pool deck again.

And forget the beach. When my best friend had her birthday party at the Greenwich beach, I wasn't allowed to go."

And how she'd wanted to. All the other kids in her class had buzzed about what fun they'd had the next Monday.

"What did you do with that dream?"

"There were still dolphins that needed trainers, so I snuck back to the pool and tried to teach myself how to swim."

"Which ended with . . ."

The sight of the water closing over her head and the bubbles rising uselessly to the surface flashed to her mind. The feeling of her lungs begging for oxygen, the burning as she swallowed the chlorinated water. Then everything had gone black. "Another ride to the hospital."

He cupped her cheek, running his thumb around the edge of her ear and tucking her hair back. "I'm glad there was someone there to save you."

"Me too." She managed a mirthless laugh. "But it scared me. It was . . ." She inhaled deeply.

"You thought dreams were dangerous."

She nodded. "They are. If I don't care, I won't get hurt."

"But you do care."

She looked down, but he nudged her chin up with his thumb until she met his gaze.

"You do. I've seen the way you care about those kids, all that you've done to give them a joy-filled Christmas season. I see the way you honor Aretha and help Marie." He glanced over his shoulder toward the dining room. "Even the way you serve me and Ruby breakfast every morning."

"It was a trade-off—it was so I could use the inn's oven."

"But you could have done the bare minimum. You could have served us leftovers. Eggs every day. You could have put frozen waffles in the toaster."

She snorted. "I couldn't do that to you—not to anyone."

"Because you don't give up on people. You may give up on stringed instruments and life-threatening sports. But you don't give up on people. You love and care for them better than anyone I've ever met."

His words made her eyes burn. If he only knew the truth. But she could barely shake her head and insist he understand how wrong he was. "I don't. Not really."

"Yes. Really. How long have you known Marie?"

"Um, almost ten years. Since she moved here. But that was just in passing at church and around town. It wasn't until Caden opened the inn's kitchen to a bunch of high school students to teach us how to cook that I really got to know her. And then when Caden came back for the summer seasons, I would stop by and help."

"Because you like cooking?"

She thought about it for a long moment. "Because I like Caden and Marie, and I wanted to be like them when I grew up. They're the best people I know." She stood up a little straighter, and his hands dropped to her shoulders, then slid down to her wrists until he twined their fingers together. "I didn't care what we were cooking or how we were cooking it. I just wanted to sit on one of those stools and listen to them talk about their lives. I wanted to hear their stories and pretend that I would be brave like them when I was older. And here I am, a fully grown adult and barely a shadow of the women they are."

"That's not true. You're wise and kind and—"

"I'm really not."

Leaning his forehead against hers, he lifted her hands to his mouth, where his patchy five o'clock shadow bristled against her knuckles. "I haven't misunderstood you."

Her stomach swooped, and her head spun. She'd waited a lifetime to hear everything he was saying. Yet he didn't really know her.

Whitney opened her mouth to tell him the whole terrible truth, but before she could speak, the bell on the swinging door jingled. Daniel pressed her knuckles briefly to his lips, then quickly stepped away as Ruby sashayed into the kitchen, her mouth already running a mile a minute.

nineteen

IN THE BACK SEAT of Whitney's SUV, Daniel looked up from his phone only to realize Ruby was still talking. She hadn't stopped since they'd left the inn that morning, and honestly, he wasn't sure what she'd been saying.

Offering a grunt of general agreement set her off again.

"Aretha said you're staying on the island through Christmas. Is that right? Well, when you're back in the city, I know this great Indian place. We should definitely get dinner sometime. I can introduce you to my friend who works at All Terrain. I mean, you'll probably meet him as soon as you start at the office. When is that? I'm sure you'll be so busy, but a man's got to eat, right? And this place is so good. Authentic and so spicy it'll make you sweat. You just have to try it."

Glancing at the rearview mirror, he caught Whitney's eye and offered a quick smile. She looked like she was fighting a grin and quickly averted her gaze back to the road.

He went back to checking emails from his new job. For someone not yet officially on payroll, he sure had a lot of them. Questions from the CEO about when he would submit his budget-savings plan. Questions from the finance team members about if empty positions were ever going to be filled. Or worse—cut. Questions from district managers about ways to increase revenue.

All this, four days before Christmas. Of course, this was the busiest season of the year for retail. But it was also supposed to be a time for family and friends, to stop and ponder the Christ child born in a manger. This was what church pageants and Christmas carols were about, right?

If this was what his new job demanded of him in his personal email, he already dreaded seeing his work email.

It was what he'd signed up for. But that had been before Whitney. Before he'd wanted to figure out how to fit someone else into his life.

Now he did. He just didn't know what that would look like. Or where she'd be. They'd been interrupted by Ruby in the kitchen the day before, before he could ask Whitney what she was going to do. If she wasn't going to culinary school, what did she see next for her life? And was he part of it?

He sure hoped so.

After turning off his phone, he tucked it into his pocket and watched the back of Whitney's head as they wound their way down two-lane roads bordered by white-dusted pines. A hurricane the year before had downed many of the majestic trees, and their remains were hidden beneath piles of pristine snow that glittered in the morning sun.

Every now and then the sun would catch a highlight in Whitney's hair, and he'd have to fight the urge to wind it around his finger. Then he'd catch a word or two that Ruby said and remember that they weren't alone. And that Ruby thought they were having a conversation.

He grunted in response to nothing in particular, and Ruby turned to him, her face aglow. "I know, right?"

He had no idea what he'd agreed with but forced a smile in response.

"You seem so much happier lately. Aretha was really worried about you, but I told her, I said, 'He'll come out of his shell. It's probably just the travel and time zone change.' It always throws me for a loop too."

Whitney let out a low chuckle but then covered it with a cough. Ruby didn't seem to notice and chattered away as the main highway led them right into town. They went as far as the street did, then turned onto a narrow road between homes on the right and an oceanfront boardwalk on the left.

He didn't know what this island's fascination with boardwalks was, but every town seemed to have one. Each as beautiful and serene as the last. Whitney parked along the road, and when he got out, the burst of cold air rushed through him, welcome and invigorating. For a moment he considered making Poppy Donaldson wait so he could sit on one of the benches facing the ocean and just enjoy the smell of sea and ice and wood-burning stoves from the nearby houses.

But Ruby reached his side before he could move, her hand slipping into his elbow and holding him close, her other hand clasping the folder of documents for Poppy. "Sure is cold this close to the water." She let out an exaggerated shiver and sidled even closer to him.

Whitney had stepped out of the car too, and she stood next to the closed door, hands in her pockets. Her nostrils flared, and she blinked several times. But she said nothing. She only punched her hands deeper into her pockets.

He couldn't tell if she was trying to communicate something to him or if she was fighting off the chill. "Are you going to be all right?" he asked.

Ruby didn't give her time to answer. "We shouldn't be

too long," she said, effectively dismissing Whitney. With a glance in each direction, she towed him across the empty street toward a two-story pink house. Its boxy shape didn't match its bubble-gum exterior, but it seemed just the type of home that someone named Poppy would own.

Ruby rapped swiftly on the turquoise door, which opened almost immediately with a warm greeting from the surprisingly young woman there.

Daniel managed one quick look over his shoulder to see Whitney standing all by herself on the boardwalk before he was whisked into the cozy warmth of a quilting haven.

The young woman at the door closed it softly behind them before moving to stand in front of a crackling fire in the hearth and pulling a phone from her pocket. This couldn't possibly be Poppy, the techno-averse artisan who still owned a fax machine.

"My grandma will be right back. She said you can look around."

That tracked.

He nodded as he perused Poppy's current projects. Three quilts were stretched on large wooden frames that dominated the room. A peek down a narrow hall suggested the frames dominated the whole house. A two-foot Christmas tree on a table in the corner couldn't compete.

Each of the frames was nearly two meters wide and almost as tall, and held an intricately designed quilt top stacked over batting and a mostly solid panel of cloth for the back. The edges were still rough, but the beauty was already there. One quilt featured red cloth jutting out into blue—clearly the beach—and a myriad of yellow fabrics shooting out from a round sun on the horizon.

He turned to show Whitney how beautiful it was, but she

wasn't there, and he could have kicked himself for allowing Ruby to pull him away from her. She was the reason that they were even meeting with Poppy—that any of the quilters had been offered a fair deal.

And she was off staring at the real ocean instead of seeing it represented in fabric.

"Everyone gravitates to that one."

He looked up as an old woman shuffled in from the kitchen. Her shoulders were stooped, and her white hair was pulled into a thin knot at the base of her neck. Age spots covered her face, and her hands looked riddled with arthritis. Her skin and eyes were so pale that the only thing bright about her was her yellow terry-cloth tracksuit.

"Thanks for waiting on me," she huffed as she slowly covered the distance between them. "Had to take some chicken soup to my neighbor, who's ailing. Don't tell nobody that he can't take care of himself, but he's not as young as he used to be."

Daniel smothered a chuckle, wondering just how old the man must be, given Poppy's advanced years. She was ninety at least. Maybe more. But she grinned with as much joy as Julia Mae.

"I'm Daniel Franklin." He held out his hand, but she swatted it away, her fingers never quite unfurling.

"Sure, sure. Figured you were Aretha's family. She eyes my spreads the same way."

"Your *spreads*?"

"Well, I suppose when they're done, they'll be spread across someone's bed or the back of a chesterfield. Don't you think?"

"Yes, ma'am."

"I've been working on this one for nearly three years now."

His stomach dropped. Less than a thousand dollars for three years of work—and that didn't include the supplies to make the thing. He gulped at the reality, and she chuckled.

"Boy, we—none of us—make 'em to make money. We make 'em 'cause they're beautiful. We make 'em 'cause we can put a little bit of ourselves out there into the world. Because in a few generations, someone's great-grandbaby is going to learn to crawl on something we made."

She leaned in closer to the stretched fabric and ran a gnarled finger along an intricate pattern of tiny stitches. He'd missed it before but realized now that only a corner of the quilt top had been sewn together, the white thread forming a pattern of perfect little sunbursts.

"Figured I'd better work on something a little more seasonal this time of year though." Poppy easily slid the front rack to the side to reveal a vibrant blue and silver piece of art. Fabric had been cut and sewn into multisided star shapes, the colors ebbing and flowing from star to star. And holding it together was silver thread in an endless row of precisely stitched five-pointed stars. Each a unique size, but somehow making a perfect decorative pattern.

"Do you do this by hand?"

Poppy's granddaughter snorted. "She won't get rid of her landline. No way she'd buy a sewing machine."

"Hush now, you." Turning back to him, Poppy dropped her voice to share her secret. "I tried one of them pedal machines, but I sew a straighter line."

"Even . . . ?" He nodded toward the swollen knuckles of her hands.

"It's not so bad so long as I keep them moving. This keeps me going."

Whitney would like Poppy, and he wished again that he'd insisted she come inside with them.

"How long have you been—"

Ruby's impatient cough stole the rest of his question. She had already settled on a small sofa that looked like it belonged in some old English estate. The papers that had been in the black folder were now spread precisely across the short coffee table, taking the place of the colorful quilting books that had occupied the space when they arrived. He looked around and found them stacked on the floor below.

That took some audacity to rearrange a person's house. Especially someone they wanted to negotiate with. That hadn't been on his mom's list of ways to interact with people, but it would have been if she'd sat in on this exchange.

Look people in the eye to show them you're listening.

Give them a firm handshake.

Don't rearrange their books without asking—even if they're not in alphabetical order.

Poppy paused at the same time he did, her eyes wide and unblinking. After a long moment of silence during which he debated with himself if she would use the word *impertinence*, Poppy finally shuffled toward the couch. "I suppose you better show me what you drove all the way down here for."

Ruby immediately launched into an explanation of the agreement to purchase Poppy's quilts directly from her instead of through the consignment agreement she had with Aretha.

Poppy nodded along as Ruby took the contract point by point. After three pages of details, she looked up at Daniel. "So, you want me to act as a wholesaler and sell you my goods at a discount? As long as I don't sell to anyone else at the same discount?"

Ruby's eyes flashed.

"Oh, don't look so surprised, girl. I've been selling things longer 'n you've been alive."

Daniel turned back to the quilts to cover his smile as Ruby and Poppy hashed out the details. Poppy asked more questions than the other quilters had, her mind clearly sharp and filled with a lifetime of business knowledge.

After several minutes, Poppy signed on the bottom line with a smile, her pen strokes a little shaky but still determined.

"Thanks for making the trip," Poppy's granddaughter said as she showed them out. "Do you need a cup of coffee for the road?"

Ruby tugged him out the door with a quick wave for Poppy. "We're fine. Maybe we'll go celebrate somewhere." As she led him across the street, the heels of her impractical boots clicking against the pavement, she gave him a broad smile. "We really should—celebrate, I mean. I can't believe we got all of them to agree to the new terms and sign off before Christmas. The sale is complete now. All we have left is for the bank to do their thing and Aretha to pass over the keys. Well, technically, she's already given me a key. But, you know, the official changing of ownership. So, what do you think?"

"About the keys?" Daniel was trying to pay attention, but he kept scanning the horizon for any sign of Whitney.

"No, not the keys." Ruby's perfect eyebrows flattened. "Celebrating. Together. We could go out for a special dinner. Just the two of us."

"The two of us?" He couldn't make sense of what she was saying. The only person he wanted to celebrate with was Whitney, and he spun slowly when he couldn't find her shape along the boardwalk.

"Daniel!" Ruby's voice was sharp. "Are you listening to me?"

"Not really." He hadn't meant to say that out loud, and her audible gasp told him he shouldn't have let it slip.

"Hey, guys!" Whitney's voice split the air, and he spun in her direction. "I'll be right there," she called, holding up a white bakery bag that he already knew held those butterscotch brownies she'd told him about. His mouth began to water at just the thought.

Ruby jerked at the cuff of his coat. "Daniel? What about dinner for two? Your aunt said you wanted to spend some time together."

"My aunt said what?" He shook his head. He didn't need her to repeat that. "Ruby, I'm . . ." His eyes darted to Whitney as she approached, her breaths coming out in little puffs of air. "I'm seeing someone."

twenty

WHEN SHE SAW Aretha's car parked in front of her shop, Whitney had to force herself not to turn into the parking lot as they returned to North Rustico. Everything inside her screamed to go directly there and leave Daniel and Ruby to find the rest of the way to the inn on their own. It wasn't far, and the boardwalk entrance was just on the other side of the end of the harbor.

But if she stopped, there would be questions she couldn't answer. One in particular. *Why?*

Whitney wasn't keen on interrupting Ruby's stunning silence with the news that Aretha had been trying to set them up for almost a month. And Whitney had been helping—oh, for money, naturally. Then she had sabotaged the whole thing by falling in love with the matchmaker's mark.

No matter how many times she repeated that in her own mind, she couldn't make it sound any prettier.

She forced herself to turn onto Harborview Drive and pulled all the way into the inn's driveway.

"Well," Ruby said, holding up the signed documents, "I suppose that was a successful trip."

Then she disappeared, slamming the car door behind her and tromping a trail through the snow in a straight shot to the red door. She didn't bother taking five extra steps to follow the shoveled path and had to shake the loose chunks from her pants on the porch.

"Well, that went well," Daniel said from the back seat.

Whitney tried to match the smile in his voice, but her face refused to budge. "I have an errand to run. I'll see you later." She rolled out of the car without waiting for his response—probably an offer to join her—shoved her hands into her pockets, and hunched her shoulders as she ran in the direction they'd come.

She was breathing hard, the cold air searing her lungs, when she reached the shop. She grabbed the handle, but it refused to budge. Smacking the door several times, she called out, "Aretha? Are you in there? It's Whitney!"

Everything inside was silent. Aretha's car was still parked off to the side of the gray-shingled building, and while the sign on the door said CLOSED, the ceiling lights shone through the angled window blinds.

"Aretha?" She pounded on the door again with her fist, but still no response.

Maybe she was in the storeroom. After hustling around the side of the small building, Whitney tried the back door. It was locked too, but she could hear movement on the other side, so she knocked hard. "Aretha? It's Whitney!"

The faded blue door swung open without notice, and Whitney had to jump back to avoid a black eye. If only Daniel had been so quick the first time she'd met him.

But this wasn't about Daniel.

Actually, yes, it was. But it was more about her and what she'd done.

"What on earth, child? You look like a hive of bees has been chasing you." Aretha paused long enough to do a head-to-toe perusal before holding open the door. "You better come in then and tell me what's going on."

Whitney nodded, unable to get any words past her labored breathing.

"You've got perfect timing. You can help me move some of these items onto the main floor." Aretha shook her head as she handed Whitney a lamp for each arm. "Jack begged off with some excuse about last-minute Christmas shopping in Charlottetown, and if I didn't know it was for me, I never would have let him go. But that man does love to buy presents." She giggled as she picked up two more fixtures. "And I do love to receive them."

Aretha led the way to the plain white door that separated the back from the store, then opened it wide enough for them to step through.

Whitney still panted like she'd run a 10K and couldn't get her brain to sort through all the words she knew in order to speak the ones she needed to. But Aretha didn't seem to mind as they carried several pieces up from the back.

"Get the other side there, would you?" Aretha pointed to a rolltop desk and grunted as she put her insubstantial weight behind it.

Whitney joined her, but the piece still didn't move.

After several attempts, Aretha brushed her hands together and sighed. "Well, that can wait for Jack or Daniel."

Leaning a hand against the desktop, Whitney swallowed through cotton and nodded, gasping for one more stabilizing breath. "Daniel," she finally pushed off her tongue.

"Yes. I'm sure he'll be by later."

"No, I need to talk with you about him."

Aretha finally stopped moving, her stillness leaving somewhat of a vacuum in the dimly lit space. But at least her silence allowed Whitney time to find the words she needed. Unzipping her coat and stuffing her mittens in her pockets, she took another breath, her lungs finally full again.

"What's going on?" Aretha asked.

"It's about Daniel—"

Aretha grabbed her hand. "Is he all right?"

"Yes. He's fine." Her face pinched painfully. "It's me. I got in the way."

"In the way of what?"

"Please," she begged. "Let me just get this out."

Aretha exaggeratedly bit her too-pink lips together, then pointed to mismatched seats with a raised eyebrow that seemed to suggest they sit.

Whitney nodded and sank into a creaky wooden chair. She prayed it didn't give out before she could say her piece. Or maybe she should pray that it did so she didn't have to.

The chair held, so she pressed on. "Daniel isn't interested in Ruby."

"Of course he is." Aretha must have realized her mistake and clamped a hand over her mouth.

"He's seeing someone."

"What?" Aretha jumped to her feet, stepping side to side as though looking for an escape from their furniture confines. "Who? Why wouldn't he tell me?"

"Because I asked him not to."

"But who is it? Someone back in Toronto?"

Scrubbing her hands down her face and holding in a painful sigh, she said, "It's me."

Aretha opened her mouth, then closed it as she fell back into her chair.

Whitney had to take the opportunity to explain or she might not get another. "After you asked me to help you set them up, I did try. But when I invited them along on activities, Daniel was interested and Ruby sometimes wasn't. And the more time I spent with him . . . He's a really great guy."

"Yes, I'm aware," Aretha said, sarcasm dripping from the short sentence.

"I couldn't help it." Her hands shook, and she tucked them under her legs, trying to get some semblance of control over her body. Her eyes and throat were already threatening a mutiny, but she couldn't break down and beg for pity when she was in the wrong. "I tried to pull back. I really did. But when I wasn't around, he came looking for me."

"So, it's his fault you went back on our agreement?"

"I never meant for it to get so out of hand. I wasn't trying to get in the way. I just—we went sledding and then the mistletoe."

Aretha crossed her arms, and hurt flashed in her eyes.

Whitney shook her head, wordlessly pleading for Aretha to understand. But it wasn't Aretha who broke the silence.

"What was the agreement?"

She jolted toward the door to the sales floor to find Daniel and Ruby, silent and still as stone. Then slowly Ruby held up a key as though that explained how they had gotten in.

But Daniel only asked his question again. "What was the agreement?"

She prayed the ocean would rise up and swallow her right then, because she couldn't handle finding out how much Daniel had heard.

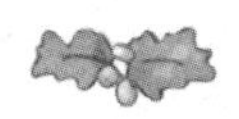

Daniel clenched his fists at his sides. His fingernails bit into his palms, a welcome distraction from the scene playing out before him and the words ringing in his ears. Aretha and Whitney had had some sort of agreement. About him.

Aretha flew across the space and grabbed his upper arms like she'd done when he was a kid. Now he had to look down at her, but she still met his gaze. "Daniel, I'm so sorry. You were just so sad, and you deserve to be happy. I love you so much that I couldn't stand to see you still hung up on Lauren."

He wasn't. He hadn't been in a while.

But that didn't matter. What mattered was, "What was the agreement?"

Whitney let out a muffled cry from where she still sat halfway into the furniture maze, head bent, hands covering her face, and hair falling forward like a veil.

Aretha glanced at Ruby, offering a half smile. "I thought you two would make a good couple. You're both so smart and savvy. You could help each other's careers. And your friends would probably get along. It just seemed so practical." She laughed softly at herself. "And as I say it, it sounds like a merger. I've never known love to make that much sense."

He felt like a broken record, but he had to know in no uncertain terms what Whitney had agreed to. He knew his aunt loved to poke her nose where it didn't always belong. But she had never been—and didn't know how to be—mean-spirited about it.

Yet Whitney had let him ramble on about Lauren, sympathized with the way he had been gaslighted. Had she been doing the same thing the whole time?

Acid bubbled in his gut, burning up his esophagus, and he crossed his arms just to apply some pressure there. "Tell me what you agreed to."

"Oh, honey."

Aretha rubbed his shoulder, but he shook off her touch. It was too much contact when all he wanted was the truth.

"I asked Whitney to help you find your way together. That's all."

"And in exchange?"

"I agreed to make up whatever she had left to earn for culinary school."

He'd almost forgotten Ruby was there, but her snort of disdain broke the silence. "You should probably do more research before you try to set people up." She tossed the black folder with the signed agreement on the table. "I'll be passing your account to one of my colleagues." She marched through the store and the door slammed behind her.

Aretha looked appropriately chagrined. "I may have suggested to her a few times that you were shy. Interested, just shy."

"Aretha." He rubbed his hands over his hair, tugging on it until the pain cleared his mind. "Why?"

"I hear how stupid it sounds with my own ears now, but I just wanted you to be happy."

"Yeah, well . . ." He glanced over her shoulder, expecting to find Whitney, but the room was empty. She'd escaped. Just like he was going to.

Because whatever he'd thought they had was not real. It couldn't be after this.

And if he hurried, he could get on the same flight off the island as Ruby.

twenty-one

WHITNEY LISTENED for the front door as she packed up the handful of spices and empty fruit trays left in the inn's kitchen. She wanted to rush through, erasing any evidence that she'd even been there. If she could get out before Aretha came by, maybe she could avoid an ugly confrontation.

And hide in her home for the next few years?

Or worse, end up with a very public dressing down?

She squeezed her eyes shut and swallowed the lump lodged in her throat. It was better to be yelled at within the privacy of the inn—while Seth and Marie and their kids were still out. She'd heard Ruby and Daniel both charge into the inn, gather their things, and flee the scene. And she'd hidden in the mudroom like the coward she was. Any apology now would be far too little, much too late. So she'd huddled inside her parka on a step stool, hugging her knees to her chin and trying to hold back the storm that threatened to burst inside her.

Now she scurried about the kitchen, wiping down every counter and leaving it just as spotless as Caden would. But she'd wait for Aretha. She may hate every second of being scolded—made worse because she knew she deserved it. But she'd take the less painful option where they were alone and she could go home after, curl up in bed, and stay there for a very long time.

Aretha didn't keep her waiting long. As soon as the front door opened, she called out, "Whitney? Are you here?"

"In the—in the kitchen." She pulled out a stool and leaned on it, then shoved it back under the island counter. She'd need something more stable if she was going to withstand the storm surge. In the end, she bolstered herself in the corner of the counter between the stove and the sink.

A moment later, Aretha sailed through the swinging door, her long coat open and the tassels on the end of her scarf dancing. "Well, I really mucked that up, didn't I?" she huffed.

Ears already ringing, Whitney thought she'd misheard her. "I'm so sorry."

"You're sorry?" Aretha looked down her nose, and Whitney shrank under the weight of it. "My dear girl, I'm the old fool here. Not you."

"You—no—it's—what?" Her bottom lip refused to stop trembling, and she couldn't stop blinking against the fire at the backs of her eyes.

"You look like you think I'm going to eat you for dinner."

She nodded slowly.

In a day that had been full of surprises, Aretha's laughter ranked at the very top—one of the sweetest sounds. "Come on." She held out her gloved hand. "Let's sit down and get comfortable."

Whitney reached for her outstretched fingers, then dropped her arm back to her side. But she followed Aretha through the dining room and into the parlor, where they shrugged out of their jackets. She slid into the corner of the sofa, letting the cushions swallow her. Hoping Aretha would sit on the opposite side.

She didn't. She chose the middle seat, angling her knees in and resting her hands on her lap. With a deep breath, Aretha offered a sad smile. "I've been reminded by no less than three people I love what an absolute clown I've been."

"Three?" Did that many people know about her involvement?

"Daniel, Marie, and my Jack."

She cringed. Marie had promised to keep it to herself, but the truth was clearly public knowledge now.

Whitney tucked her legs under her and wrapped her arms around her stomach, wishing she'd never taken off her jacket. At least that afforded her a modicum of protection. Even if it was imaginary.

"I got so caught up in my plan for Daniel that I failed to see what was happening right under my nose." Aretha smiled conspiratorially. "He fell in love with you."

"No. It wasn't like that. We were just—"

"Oh, don't try to lie to me again."

"I didn't mean to. I'm so sorry. I feel so awful. I swear that I didn't mean to come between him and Ruby. I didn't have any of those feelings for him at the beginning, when you first suggested it. I mean, I thought he was handsome, but that was it. It's just that . . ." She pinched her eyes closed and tried not to picture Daniel's smile or the barely-there dimple that showed up when he thought something was really funny. "He bought this ridiculous turkey hat at the farmers' market in Summerside, and then he *wore* it. And I knew there was more to him than he wanted to reveal, but maybe he'd show me some of who he really was."

Aretha stifled a chuckle. "How could you not fall in love with a turkey hat?"

"I didn't fall—" But she couldn't get the lie past her lips without releasing a flood of tears that choked her throat and rained down her cheeks.

Aretha patted her hand. "It's all right. You don't have to apologize for loving Daniel. Or pretend you don't. I love that boy like we're blood—even though I'm only related to him through my ex-husband. Daniel has always been one of my favorite parts of the Franklin family. Even as a boy, he was special. He wasn't like his cousins, but he tried harder than anyone I know to demonstrate love. He'd come hug me, and I'd hear him counting in my ear to ten. Once I asked him why to ten, and he told me it was so I'd know he wanted to be there."

Whitney's tears increased at the idea of young Daniel doing everything in his power to love and be loved—even if it looked like checking off a list of requirements. And adult Daniel trying so hard to understand Lauren but never being able to. Because she had never loved the real him. She'd never seen he was worthy of her love.

But oh, how he was. Worthy of every ounce that Lauren—or anyone else—had to offer.

Her lips trembled too much to respond, and Aretha pulled her into a warm embrace. "Oh, honey. It's all right," she whispered.

"I ruined your plan and your—"

Aretha released her and leaned back to look directly into her face. "You get that out of your head right now. My plan was always and only for Daniel to be happy."

"Like I said," she garbled through a watery laugh. "I ruined the plan."

"Well . . . he may not be happy at the moment, but my prayer for him has always been for the long term."

Right. He'd be happy again because he'd find joy again. He'd gotten over Lauren. He'd certainly get over her. And some lucky girl would recognize how special he was.

She stared toward the ceiling and blew into her eyes to keep the tears at a minimum.

"Are you going to go to Charlottetown after the New Year?" Aretha asked.

Whitney shook her head. "I didn't make enough for tuition, and they won't save my spot."

Aretha sat up straight, her neck like steel. "You held up your part of our agreement. I'll give you whatever you need to cover your tuition."

"You can't do that."

Aretha looked offended. "I beg your pardon. I just sold my store for a very fair price, and I can do whatever I so choose with that money. And if I choose to give some of it to a worthy student, then that's my choice. No one can tell me otherwise."

Whitney's own chuckle surprised her. "I'm not going to go. I'd already decided. It's not . . . it's not only the money."

Aretha leaned forward, eyes intense. "What is it then?"

"It's something Daniel said. He has me thinking about my dream."

"And what is that?"

Whitney chewed on her thumbnail as she stared beyond Aretha's shoulder. "I'm not sure yet. But I'm going to figure it out."

"What are you going to do about Daniel?"

The back of her throat convulsed, and she thought she was going to be sick. "What can I do except try to forget him?" The question tasted like rotten eggs.

Aretha gave a very unladylike snort. "Oh, no. That'll never do. When you love someone, you give them a little time to cool down. Then you go after them, and you show them how much joy you bring to their life. Because you did that for Daniel. He's hurt. He feels the sting right now, but in a few days, he's going to realize how dark his world is without you in it."

With a squeeze of her hand, Aretha grinned. "So, are you going to be in it?"

Whitney needed a dream.

Simple. No problem. Just a lifelong goal. No pressure.

Something she could pursue without fear. Something worthwhile. Something that wasn't liable to nearly kill her.

Because she wanted to be brave. But she didn't need to be stupid.

Okay. No problem. Dream.

On her own sofa, she tucked her crossed legs beneath her. The simple string of white Christmas lights around her window burned even against her closed eyes. But the mini bulbs didn't illuminate any brilliant ideas.

Maybe it was too quiet. Yes. That was definitely the problem.

She hopped up and turned her phone to a Christmas playlist. Jingling bells and all that. Certainly that would inspire an idea.

Ten minutes later, she wasn't convinced. Maybe walking would help.

She popped up and paced the tiny perimeter of her bungalow's living room.

In high school, one of her friends had put together a vision board—pictures clipped from magazines and pasted to a big board of dreams. Angie's had looked like a "where in the world are celebrities taking holiday this week?" Infinity pools and crystal-clear water. White beaches and white stucco homes built into Greek hills. Even ten years later, Angie still talked about the exotic places she wanted to vacation. Though her destinations were more informed by her favorite travel personality on TikTok now—Cruising with Cretia or something like that.

Whitney didn't dream about far-flung travels or exotic anything.

So what did she dream about? What would she put on her vision board?

The white poster board in her mind's eye remained blank. Except for one face.

Daniel's.

Nope. She'd screwed that up way too much for him to come within a hundred kilometers of her dream board.

But his words drifted through her mind. "*You don't give up on people.*" He'd said that when she'd told him about sitting in Caden's kitchen and soaking up whatever Caden could teach her. Whitney may not know what she wanted to *do*, but she knew the kind of person she wanted to *be*. Brave and kind and willing to try.

Caden had embodied that as long as she'd known her. She'd gone from being an assistant in her dad's bakery to being the inn's chef to launching an after-school cooking program for teenagers in Toronto with the Cooking Network star Jerome Gale.

Whitney didn't need to have the same journey. But maybe Caden could inspire something more than a dream of travel.

Something more like investing in a younger generation. After all, that was what Caden had done for her.

Before Whitney could come up with a reason not to or let herself focus on the challenges, she snatched up her phone and pressed the screen to connect her call.

Caden answered on the second ring. "Whitney? What a pleasant surprise!"

A baby wailed on the other end to say he was much less pleased.

"Sorry. Hang on." Caden dropped her voice to coo at her little one. "Hush now, AJ. Here you go. Drink your bottle."

Whitney drummed her fingers on the leg of her flannel pajama pants. This was probably a terrible idea. Caden was clearly busy.

But you've helped everyone else this season. Why can't you be a help to Caden too?

The voice in her head sounded an awful lot like Daniel. So instead of apologizing to Caden for calling and then hanging up like her old voice would tell her to do, she took a deep breath and waited.

"Sorry. Adam Jr. gets cranky when his feeding schedule gets off. He's a lot like his dad in that way." Caden chuckled at her own joke.

From the far side of the phone, Adam hollered, "Do not," which only made Caden laugh harder.

"Whitney," she said. "It's great to hear from you. What have you been up to?"

"Baking pies mostly. Selling them at farmers' markets."

"I bet you've been a hit across the island."

Whitney made a noncommittal sound but let the compliment wash over her anyway. "So, I've been . . . I'm not sure what I'm going to do next."

"Really? What do you want to do?"

"Work with you?" It came out as more of a question than she'd meant it, so she cleared her throat and said it again. "I want to work with you."

Caden's laughter pealed through the phone, and Whitney cringed. She'd said something wrong, and this was where she threw in her shin guards or violin bow and ran for cover. This was when she turned around at the edge of the pool, picked up her towel, and sat back down in the bleachers.

But not today.

"You have no idea what an answer to prayer you are," Caden said. "I mean, you're pretty much a Christmas miracle. I've only told one other person that we need to hire help."

"Wh-what?"

"Jerome wants to expand the program, and I haven't told him yet, but I'm pregnant again." Caden's smile came through loud and clear.

"Again?"

"I told him I needed to find some full-time help. Are you looking for full-time work? It doesn't matter. I'll make it work. I just—I need someone I can trust implicitly."

"But I'm not that good of a cook."

With a laugh that brushed all concerns aside, Caden said, "Yes, you are. Marie told me if I ever decided not to come back to the inn for the summer season, she was going to snap you up."

Whitney couldn't form words as warmth wrapped around her, better than the softest throw.

"Now, I'm coming back, mind you. But I could sure use your help. It's a lot of administration and lesson planning and teaching and simply encouraging these kids to keep trying. Can you do that?"

Because of Daniel, she nodded. She didn't give up on people. "I can."

"Oh, but the job has to be in Toronto. Are you looking to move?"

She couldn't get the word out fast enough. "Yes."

Thirty minutes later, Whitney sat on her sofa in stunned silence, her cheeks hurting from the breadth of her smile. She didn't exactly have a dream. But she absolutely had a plan. She had a confirmed job offer, temporary housing, and the chance to work with two of the best chefs she'd ever met.

She wasn't afraid that she'd jump ship or fail to live up to anyone's expectations. Like Daniel had said, she didn't give up on her friends. Caden trusted her to do this job, the same way Marie and Seth had trusted her with their kids.

She could be Caden's Christmas miracle—and Caden could be hers too.

If Christmas miracles were being passed around, she sent up a prayer for one more. Taking a deep breath, she asked for the words to explain, words that would touch his heart. Then she began her text.

twenty-two

DANIEL GLARED at his laptop, paced the length of his living room, then glared at it again. He couldn't seem to make it through an email or a spreadsheet without his mind wandering back to the island. Specifically, to one golden-haired liar.

No. Nope. Not going there.

He was not going to think about her anymore. He had a job to get ready for and a world that did not involve her. Or the sweet smell of cinnamon and sugar that seemed to follow her wherever she went.

He clasped his fist to his chest, forcing himself to take a few deep breaths. Or he could put it through a wall.

His landlord would not appreciate that.

After taking another deep breath, he released the tension in his hand as he released the air through his nose.

Not great. But better.

He marched a few steps but stopped when he realized he was stomping on the ceiling of the apartment below. They probably thought he was trying to break through. But even that wouldn't take away the ache in his chest. It might distract him for a minute, though.

Huffing out a sigh, he tiptoed to the brown corduroy sofa that dominated the space and flopped onto it. If Christmas was a season for giving gifts and God was the giver of all good gifts, what did that make Whitney?

She had set up residence in his brain and refused to leave. From the time he'd boarded the airplane in Charlottetown to this moment, he'd had no relief—no reprieve. The woman was stuck in his brain. Not in a *good gifts* kind of way. It was more a constant reminder of what he'd never have in his life again.

Memories of her flooded through him. Her smile. Her laughter. The way she trusted him to guide their sled safely. The comfort in her hugs. The way her forehead would crinkle when she tried to understand something.

Her kiss.

He'd thought he'd known her. He'd thought he'd seen her. No pretense. No lies.

He'd been so wrong.

Whitney had been different from Lauren—maybe because she knew about Lauren. He'd been careful to confirm that he wasn't misreading the situation, misinterpreting her actions. He'd trod slowly, cautiously.

And it had blown up in his face, just like his relationship with Lauren.

The pain was different, though. With Lauren he'd been filled with anger, then frustration until it simmered to a low boil. Eventually, it had evaporated, leaving little evidence. Just a cautionary reminder to tread lightly.

But Whitney had left a hole—an aching chasm somewhere in the vicinity of his heart. He was having trouble finding that now too.

He could be patient if he thought the pain would slowly subside, but how was he supposed to fill an emptiness that only Whitney fit?

"Argh!" He grabbed his lone throw pillow and stuffed it against his face, lest his downstairs neighbors think he had released an angry grizzly in the building.

A knock on his door made him jump to his feet. Probably said neighbors checking to make sure his apartment was still standing.

The building? Yes. The tenant? Barely.

He flung the door open. A silver-haired man held out a white bag filled with Styrofoam takeout containers.

Right. Thai food. Dinner. He'd ordered it an hour before when he'd been hungry and significantly less angsty.

"It's $24.70."

Daniel nodded and reached for the entry table, where he always unloaded his keys, phone, and wallet when he walked in the door. His keys were in the bowl. But his wallet and phone were conspicuously absent.

He quickly patted down the front and back pockets of his jeans—trying not to think about how he'd gotten used to a more casual uniform around Whitney. They were empty.

"Um . . ." He spun around slowly. "Hang on. I've got it around here somewhere."

The delivery guy nodded, lowering the bag to his side as he leaned a shoulder to the doorframe. "No problem. Take your time. You're my last delivery of the day."

"Huh?" Daniel wasn't so much asking for clarification as he was filling the silence, checking the kitchen counters and the table.

But the guy didn't need much encouragement to keep

going. "Your place looks like mine. Who needs decorations when the rest of the city is overflowing with them, eh?"

Daniel snapped his head up from where he'd been looking under the couch. "What?"

"No tree. No garland."

He hadn't needed any. Marie had made the inn as festive as he could want. The tree had been trimmed, the kids' fingerprints all over it. Ribbons and bows and stockings hung from the mantel. The mistletoe hung in just the right spot.

Pain ripped through his chest.

Stupid mistletoe.

"You done with your Christmas shopping or going out tonight? It's Christmas Eve, you know."

He blinked at the guy, the date not quite registering. "No." He didn't care how the guy took that response, turning back to the hunt for his wallet. It wasn't stuck between the sofa cushions. Or on any of the shelves of his bookcase.

Spinning around with his hands on his hips, he scowled at every corner of the room. It wasn't an overly large space. In fact, most would consider it small. And up until that moment, he'd have considered it clean and organized. But his system had clearly failed him.

Daniel should have used the app and paid the service fee. Contact-free delivery sounded pretty good right about now. And at this rate, the guy would invite himself in to share the pad Thai before Daniel found his wallet.

"Hang on," he mumbled as he stomped into the lone bedroom and rummaged through the jeans he'd thrown in the hamper the night before. There. That wasn't fabric. He dug into a pocket and pulled out his phone.

Out of habit, he touched the screen, and it lit up to reveal a series of texts. All from Aretha.

I'm so sorry. This was all my fault. I only wanted you to be happy.

We miss you! Please come back for Christmas at least.

Whitney is miserable. Did you get her message?

He shoved the phone into the pocket of the pants he was wearing, ignoring the tug inside him at his aunt's appeal and the urge to read the texts he'd been ignoring for several days. Then he resumed his search for his wallet. He'd settle for a couple loose twenties at this point.

The laundry basket yielded nothing else, so he threw himself on the floor and peered under his bed. There it was. He must have kicked it there by accident the night before. He hadn't slept well since getting back to Toronto, and he had been nearing zombie conditions when he'd fallen into bed.

After snatching the brown leather bump, he hopped back up and started toward the front door.

"Us bachelors have a lot of freedom this time of year, eh?" the delivery guy said.

Us?

The bottom of his stomach dropped out, and in a flash Daniel saw his future in the other man's eyes. Alone on Christmas Eve. No one even to share a takeout meal with. No one to give gifts to. No one to give him a gift.

No hugs from sticky little arms. No one to snuggle with in front of a fire or stroll with through the neighborhood, holding hands.

Daniel ripped out two bills and shoved them at the delivery guy.

"Hey!" The guy's eyes lit up. "Merry Christmas, man!"

He must have tipped more than he'd planned. Certainly

more than he would have spent on the app. But he didn't care. He just wanted the guy gone and some peace and quiet with his chicken and noodles.

And no more reminders of Whitney and the island and what Christmas could be.

He dumped his food onto one of the three plates he owned and stood at the kitchen counter, eyeing it wearily. He twirled his fork into it but paused with the food halfway to his mouth before letting it drop to the plate with a clatter.

This was a foretaste of every holiday for the rest of his life.

No joy. No spark. No Whitney.

There are plenty of other women in the city.

But there was no one like her. There never would be. Besides, he didn't want anyone else. He just wanted Whitney. He wanted a life with her. He wanted her laughter and her tears and kids with frenzied curls just like their mom's.

He would put them on his shoulders when they walked around the zoo gawking at the strange and wild animals, and he would help them with their math homework. He would love their mom so much that they would never have to wonder.

She would help him see the world clearly. She would nudge him in the right direction and interpret what didn't make sense.

And he'd help her find her dream.

Leaning his elbows on the counter and pressing his face into his hands, he sighed heavily.

He had only two options. A future with Whitney. Or one without.

A future filled with hope. Or bleakness.

But he wasn't sure he could trust her.

Aretha had tried to manipulate his love life—but she'd thought she was helping him. Her goal had always been his happiness. He had no trouble believing that. She'd always been the type to have a plan for his life.

That didn't explain why Whitney had been part of it all. But maybe she had thought she was helping too.

He grabbed his phone and opened his text messages. The little red number in the corner said 9. He hated those alerts.

But he hadn't been ready to read her messages. Until now.

Hi. It's me. I'm sorry. I know that can't be enough, but I'll keep saying it until you believe it. I messed up so badly. And I hate that I hurt you. That's the very last thing I would ever want to do.

I'd barely met you when your aunt asked me to help her get you and Ruby together. You seemed sad. Maybe a little lonely. And I knew that Aretha only wanted your happiness. I thought that maybe helping her could solve both of our problems—my tuition and your happiness. I told myself it wasn't a good idea, but Aretha was so sure Ruby was exactly what you needed.

Then we started spending time together. And, well, you know.

The day that Ruby announced she'd gotten R & R to agree to the new terms, she kissed you. And I was beyond jealous. I tried to avoid you, tried to put some space between us. But I missed you. I missed the little lines you get above your nose when you're thinking. I missed the way you are with Julia Mae. I missed the humor that you only shared with me.

It was the day we went sledding. I realized that I didn't want you to be with Ruby. I wanted you to be with me. I still do.

You are everything I never knew I needed in my life. No one has ever challenged and encouraged me the way you do. You never made fun of me for not having a dream but refused to let me settle for living without one.

I'm so sorry that I didn't tell you about my arrangement with Aretha. I'm sorry that I made you doubt my feelings—or worse, your own. I didn't tell you the whole truth, but I promise you that I never lied about what I feel for you.

You are a good man. And if you ever decide to give me a second chance, I wouldn't give you another reason to question my feelings.

If you don't, well, I'm so glad to have known you. Thank you for trusting me with your story. Lauren messed up. And I would know. I did too.

Daniel sat back, scratching at his whiskers and blinking against a burning in his eyes as he stared at her words. Scrolling through them again to make sure he hadn't missed something, he took a deep breath.

If what Whitney had said was true, she'd been caught up in Aretha's plan and the offer to help her pay for culinary school. She'd been convinced that Aretha knew what he needed.

He smiled to himself. Aretha was a bit of a force of nature.

Whitney is miserable.

He could relate.

Maybe if they were both morose on their own, they could find something else together.

Even little Julia Mae had known that the true meaning of Christmas was that they were never meant to be alone. And human love—well, that could be a reflection of God's forgiveness.

Even he—who so often misunderstood or couldn't read a situation—was created for relationship.

And the only person he wanted a relationship with was Whitney.

Scrolling through his phone, he found the app he needed. And with a few taps, he purchased a ticket for the first flight in the morning, which departed in a little more than six hours. Then he headed for his bedroom and shoveled clothes into his duffle, ignoring the rapidly cooling pad Thai on his counter. He'd probably regret that later. But he couldn't be distracted with trivial things when he had a trip to take.

Zipping up his bag, he almost tossed it toward the front door. Then he had an idea. He jogged back into his room, found one more special item, and tucked it into the bag.

He couldn't show up on the island without it.

twenty-three

WHITNEY CALLED her mom and dad on Christmas Eve. It took her only two tries to tell them that she had decided not to move to Charlottetown. Her mom panicked. Her dad reminded her that he was not going to cover her bills while she tried to figure out what to do next.

She bit her tongue and didn't tell him that she hadn't asked him to.

When she told them she was moving to Toronto to work with Caden after the New Year and had already arranged to live in Caden and Adam's one-bedroom basement apartment for at least the first six months, they turned strangely quiet. No string of questions or nervous titters.

"I'll be making a good salary," she said. "Enough to cover rent, city life, and even put some into savings."

After a very long pause, her mom asked, "But you've never lived in a city. Why Toronto?"

Because of Daniel. Because he'd reminded her of what Caden had confirmed. She was a trusted part of this community, and she showed up for the people in her life. The people she chose and the ones who chose her.

She wasn't flaky with her friends. And they recognized that. They counted on her for that. Maybe she didn't know what she wanted to do with the rest of her life, but she knew where she wanted to be. With the people who loved her just as she was.

Her smile sounded in her voice as she responded to her mom's question. "Because I have friends there who believe in me."

And if she apologized enough, Daniel might still be counted among them.

Aretha had given her a tiny seed of hope that maybe he could forgive her. Maybe he still felt the way he had before.

Even without that hope, she'd be on her way to Toronto for the chance to work with Caden. With it, she couldn't get there fast enough.

But her parents didn't need to know about Daniel yet. She wasn't ready to have them pepper her with questions or sow doubt where she didn't have answers. In the right time, she'd tell them about the man who had stolen her heart.

First, she had to find out if she still had his.

She'd booked her plane ticket for three days after Christmas. Aretha said he might need a week. Whitney wanted to be there the moment he was ready.

She'd planned to spend Christmas in Charlottetown, but Little Jack had begged her to stay in North Rustico to see him perform, and she couldn't miss her last chance to do so. She'd happily accepted Marie's invitation to join their family at the inn for a big turkey dinner.

All the tables in the dining room had been pushed together into a single form that would have rivaled any from a period drama. Even the decor felt like it was meant only for special occasions. Crystal-studded silver rings held navy cloth napkins stretched across plates of fine white china with silver-dipped edges. The silver candelabra in the center of the table housed five white candles, each burning brightly despite the vibrant sunlight streaming through the row of white-framed windows against the blue wall.

Marie had never claimed to be a cook, but she'd followed a few of Caden's recipes to bring some of the island's favorite delights to the table. Next to the big golden bird sat a dish of oyster stuffing and another of scalloped potatoes, crisp around the edges and so creamy in the middle. Aretha had brought meat pies and seafood chowder.

And, of course, Whitney had provided the last of her lattice-topped apple pies.

She sat down across from Little Jack, his fork and knife already in hand and sticking straight up on either side of his plate. Seth sat at the head of the table, Marie to his left and Jessie's high chair between them. Julia Mae and Little Jack completed the row. Aretha and Big Jack sat on the right side, which left an empty chair at the foot of the table. Every time her gaze strayed in that direction, Whitney couldn't help but see Daniel's face there and wonder if he was all alone. If he'd gotten her text. If he'd deleted it before reading it.

"Can we eat now?" Little Jack asked, clunking his silverware against the pristine tablecloth.

"We pray first," Seth said. Without any additional preamble, he bowed his head and said a quick prayer of thanksgiving for the Lord's goodness and mercy, which they remembered especially on this day, when they celebrated the birth of his Son, Jesus.

Everyone looked up with big smiles on their faces. Plates were filled, and even Julia Mae was quiet as she dug into her food.

After several minutes of the only sound being the clatter of cutlery, Seth looked at his son. "What are you most excited for in the pageant this afternoon?"

Little Jack shoved a bite of turkey into his cheek and spoke around it. "That I get to be the angel."

Big Jack hummed deep in the back of his throat. "What makes the angel better than that star?"

"'Cause the angel was the first one to tell the good news."

Marie smiled proudly, and Seth squeezed his wife's hand. "Smart kid. He must get it from you."

Whitney put down her fork, abandoning the delicious meal as her stomach lurched, and she looked toward heaven with a prayer that she might have a future like that. She wasn't sure she could wait another week—or even three days—to see Daniel. She wasn't sure she *should*.

Christmas was a day to share with loved ones, and while she dearly loved this family, her heart was away on the mainland.

After the dinner was fully enjoyed and dessert equally so, they sat around the table talking of gifts they'd opened that morning and what they would do after the pageant that evening. When someone knocked on the front door, they all looked at each other as though counting to see who was missing.

Whitney could think of only one.

After shoving her chair back without a word, she raced for the red door. She flung it open and immediately burst out laughing. A man stood with his back to her, his head covered in a turkey-shaped toque.

Daniel turned around with a wide smile and tugged her by the hand onto the porch. Whitney followed easily, ignoring the cold and the gently falling snow as she closed the door behind her. She thought she heard Aretha ushering everyone into the kitchen for cleanup duty, and she made a note to thank the woman later.

"I was hoping to make you laugh," Daniel said, his eyes sweeping over her like a drowning man looking at a lifeboat.

"You definitely managed that." She chuckled. "You probably always will in that thing."

Holding her hands in his, he looked down at them and studied the backs of her fingers. "I love your laugh. In fact, I bought this silly thing because I figured you'd get a kick out of it. The funny thing is that hearing your laugh reminded me that I hadn't heard my own in a really long time. You helped me find it again. And I will never forget that."

Her bottom lip trembled, and she fought for control, not sure if she would laugh or cry or both. When she bit into it just to hold it still, his gaze followed the motion. Pressing his thumb to her lip, he tugged gently against the center.

It was almost as good as a kiss. Almost.

"I know that what I did was not okay," she said. "I'm sure it reminded you of . . . bad memories, and I am so sorry."

"I got your text," he said, and her stomach flipped all the way over. He was silent for a long time, and her mind filled in every possible terrible outcome.

"I didn't know how else to—I'm sorry that I treated you like—"

He cut her off with a quick shake of his head. "Here's the thing. You're nothing like Lauren. Not even a little bit. She never apologized. I don't think she knew how. She never saw that her actions hurt me. But I knew you were gutted from that moment at the store."

The memories rushed back, and tears flooded her eyes.

Breathing became a struggle as the weight of her mistake pressed against her chest all over again.

Her icicle fingers curled into the warmth of his palm, and he stared at the spot where his thumb rubbed a slow circle on her knuckles. She could see him working out what he wanted to say and shivered as she waited.

"I wish you had told me what you were part of."

She opened her mouth to apologize again, but he stopped her with a quick squeeze of her fingers.

"But I understand why you did what you did. And the Lord knows Aretha could talk a tomcat into a tuxedo."

Whitney giggled with a nod. There was no denying that.

Before she could say anything else, he met her gaze. "I won't lose you because of this. I've never felt so much for anyone before. I didn't even know this was possible." He slid his fingers into her hair, his palms cupping her ears. But she didn't need to hear to read the words on his lips. "I love you, Whitney."

She understood the feeling. Joy and hope and love bubbled in her chest until she didn't even feel the cold air or realize she'd forgotten her coat. Daniel was all she needed.

"I love you too," she whispered.

His smile reached across the island, but suddenly his gaze narrowed. "What are you going to do about culinary school, though?"

"I already called to take my name off their list."

"Why?"

"Because Caden offered me a job working with her and Jerome Gale."

"The TV chef?"

"Yep."

He chuckled. "And where is this dream job?"

She looked down then up with a smile. "It's in Toronto. That's what makes it my dream."

"Toronto, huh? Were you thinking you might look me up?"

"Maybe I already got your address from Aretha and looked up local stores in your neighborhood in hopes of randomly bumping into you."

"Hmm." His face fought a grin, but his dimple refused to be tamed. "Randomly, eh? Sounds more like stalking to me."

She shoved his shoulder playfully. "It's only stalking if I show up at your building. Which I wouldn't have done until the second day. At least. I promise."

"You promise you'll always stalk me?"

"I won't let you go again," she whispered as he pulled her face to his, their lips only a breath apart.

"I won't either."

The front door swung open unexpectedly, and with the burst of warmth came a cacophony that forced them to take a step back.

"Mr. Daniel, you came back for the pageant!" Julia Mae ran to him and threw her arms around his knees, pressing her cheek to him. "I knew you'd come back. Jack didn't believe me, but I knew."

He patted her knitted hat and smiled down at her. "Yeah. I'm back for the pageant." But when he looked up, the joy that sparked in his eyes was all for Whitney. "You guys go along. We'll be right there. I need Miss Whitney to show me something inside."

"What?" Julia Mae asked.

He didn't answer. Instead, he ushered her toward her family, where her dad scooped her up and Marie gave them a little wave. Aretha stood motionless, her hands clasped over her mouth.

When they were finally alone again, Whitney asked, "What did you want me to show you inside?"

Giving her a wicked grin, he whispered, "The mistletoe."

She laughed, just as he'd probably known she would. Then she led him inside toward the rest of their lives. The best yet to come.

Acknowledgments

This book is in your hands only because of God's goodness. As with nearly every book I've ever written, I got to the halfway point and wondered how it could possibly come together. How could these disparate storylines weave together into something bigger than what I had imagined on my own?

But God.

In fact, it is only by his goodness that I have dreamed bigger dreams than I dared to and watched him bring them about. If you're afraid to pursue a dream because it might be hard, may I be one reminder that worthy dreams always are. Obstacles are part of the journey. And it's worth fighting to overcome them. Keep trying. God is faithful.

Also know that you're not alone. Within this wild writing life, I've found a community that I didn't know I needed.

So much gratitude to the readers who have trekked back to the island with me over and over again. Your prayers and words of encouragement have buoyed me through dark seasons. Thank you!

Rachel Kent and Books & Such Literary Management, thank you for believing in my stories. Thank you for the way you invest in your authors and have built such an amazing community. I'm forever proud to be a Bookie!

The amazing team at Revell, you are incredible. Thank you for making this book better than I could have made it on my own. Kelsey, Jessica, Brianne, Karen, Hannah, and the rest of the team, my endless appreciation. Thank you for suggesting a return to the Red Door Inn. It's been a delight to spend my Christmas there.

The Panera ladies, my fellow writers, confidantes, and friends. You are one of the truest blessings of this writing life. I couldn't do it without you! Thank you for showing up faithfully in my life, Lindsay Harrel, Sara Carrington, Jennifer Deibel, Sarah Popovich, Erin McFarland, Ruth Douthitt, Tari Faris, Kim Wilkes, and Breana Johnson. Thank you for helping me dream big dreams and encouraging me to go after them.

My family, who still tolerates my writing schedule and gladly travels abroad when I say it's time we go back to the island. I'm so glad we got to see the beautiful red shores again. Rachel, Hannah, and Mom, thanks for making more island memories with me. I'll hold a baby goat with you any day.

I've said it before, and I'll keep repeating it: The Johnson/Whitson clan is my favorite. I'd rather sit in a hospital room with you (which we did for a month while I was supposed to be writing this book) than party with anyone else. But who am I kidding? We basically had a party on the fourteenth floor. Life is hard and filled with the unexpected, and I'm glad we choose to be there for each other.

Liz Johnson is the *New York Times* bestselling author of more than twenty novels, including *The Red Door Inn*, *Beyond the Tides*, *The Last Way Home*, and *Summer in the Spotlight*. She works in marketing, makes her home in Phoenix, Arizona, and dreams of sunny days on PEI shores. Learn more at LizJohnsonBooks.com.

Find even more sweet stories in the

PRINCE EDWARD ISLAND DREAMS SERIES

"A charming inn in need of restoration, Prince Edward Island, and a love story? Yes, please! Liz Johnson crafts a story about new beginnings and fresh hope."

—BECKY WADE,
ECPA bestselling author, on *The Red Door Inn*

a division of Baker Publishing Group
RevellBooks.com

Available wherever books and ebooks are sold.

Meet

LIZ JOHNSON

LizJohnsonBooks.com